"Mary South gets it. With dark humor, she knocks down like so many lined-up ducks all the consoling pieties that nurture humanist fiction, and sets up in their place a version of subjects irremediably mediated, strung out along networks that far exceed them. Her universe is glitchy, full of weakly encrypted memory, open-source desire, self-replicating fantasy: the human in hock to the algorithm."   —Tom McCarthy, author of *Satin Island*

"Mary South's stories are a vital mix of wry humor, cunning provocation, disturbing prophecy, and deep feeling. A brilliant and brilliantly strange and strangely funny and menacing debut!"
                                        —Sam Lipsyte, author of *Hark* and *The Ask*

"Mary South's wickedly, exquisitely hilarious collection dwells in the intimate aches of modern life, writ large in strange, delightful stories that include, but are not limited to, clones, brain surgery, internet trolls, and warehouses full of spare men. Dazzlingly imagined and full of wit, *You Will Never Be Forgotten* is a gift to readers everywhere, a ferocious transmission from one of the most audacious, most original new voices in fiction."
                                        —Alexandra Kleeman, author of *Intimations*
                                            and *You Too Can Have a Body Like Mine*

"While Mary South's stories feature the cutting-edge technology of our present and near future, what makes this collection so exceptional is the deft hand with which she can peel back the sheen of novelty to get to the core of these characters' triumphs and struggles. With sharp insight and wit, South lays bare the timeless truths of love, loss, and loneliness at the heart of these stories."
                                        —Sara Nović, author of *Girl at War*

"One of the strangest and most exciting collections I've read in recent times. This is what I hope for from speculative fiction: an unease that pulls you through the story with urgency but also delivers new formations of haunting questions that linger long after the story ends."   —Jac Jemc, author of *The Grip of It*

"This is a delicious, absurdly sharp collection of stories—funny, painful, macabre, sometimes gruesome, and humming with intelligence. Mary South is a tremendous talent and this book is a gem."
     —Lydia Kiesling, author of *Golden State*

"What a heady, delicious, devastating collection. These stories, in their limitless wit and invention, begin as satisfying intellectual puzzles and then bloom into something fiercer, wilder—expanding to contain the fullness of dread, loss, longing, shame, terror. Mary South has written a tremendous book."
     —Clare Beams, author of *The Illness Lesson*

"Here are ten stories of loneliness and loss, bristling with gallows humor and wrought of nimble, gleefully exacting sentences. With wide-reaching curiosity and deadpan wit, Mary South writes the absurdity and banality of technology-damaged life."
     —Kathryn Scanlan, author of *Aug 9—Fog*

"These swift and spiky stories dive, unafraid, into grief and violence— and emerge with insights as vivid and powerful as a lightning strike. *You Will Never Be Forgotten* is an arresting, unpredictable, and hilarious collection, and Mary South is an ingenious new talent."
     —Laura van den Berg, author of *The Third Hotel*

mary south
you will never be forgotten

Mary South is a graduate of Northwestern University and the MFA program in fiction at Columbia University. For many years, she has worked as a contributing editor at the literary journal *NOON*. She is also a former intern in *The New Yorker*'s fiction department and a Bread Loaf work-study fellow. Her writing has appeared in *The Believer*, *The Collagist*, *Conjunctions*, *Electric Literature*, *NOON*, and *Words Without Borders*, and on NewYorker.com. The writer Maile Meloy awarded her story "Not Setsuko" an honorable mention in the *Zoetrope: All-Story* fiction contest. She lives in New York City.

you will never be forgotten

you will never be forgotten

STORIES

mary south

FSG ORIGINALS | FARRAR, STRAUS AND GIROUX | NEW YORK

FSG ORIGINALS
Farrar, Straus and Giroux
120 Broadway, New York 10271

Library of Congress Cataloging-in-Publication Data
Names: South, Mary, 1982– author.
Title: You will never be forgotten : stories / Mary South.
Description: First edition. | New York : FSG Originals / Farrar, Straus
    and Giroux, 2020.
Identifiers: LCCN 2019049256 | ISBN 9780374538361 (paperback)
Classification: LCC PS3619.O883 A6 2020 | DDC 813/.6—dc23
LC record available at https://lccn.loc.gov/2019049256

Designed by Gretchen Achilles

Our books may be purchased in bulk for promotional, educational,
or business use. Please contact your local bookseller or the Macmillan
Corporate and Premium Sales Department at 1–800-221-7945, extension 5442,
or by e-mail at MacmillanSpecialMarkets@macmillan.com.

www.fsgoriginals.com • www.fsgbooks.com
Follow us on Twitter, Facebook, and Instagram at @fsgoriginals

1   3   5   7   9   10   8   6   4   2

For Andrew

contents

you will never be forgotten

keith prime

The Keiths are Keiths because they are not particularly hand-some, not particularly intelligent, not particularly kind. A Keith would never train to compete in professional sports or practice an instrument until he became a maestro. Neither would a Keith jump in front of a loaded gun, but he would help you gather the contents of your grocery bag if you spilled it on the sidewalk. On a city bus, your gaze would pass pleasantly over a Keith as though over a stretch of ocean. There are warehouses of Stephanies, warehouses of Daniels, warehouses of Mayas, Georges, Crystals, Jamals, and Nicoles, but I am in Keiths.

It's always sad when one of your Keiths is harvested. We're obligated to see it once, at orientation, a Keith scooped out like ice cream from a bucket or disassembled as a very large jigsaw puzzle. In Tibet, monks spend months making mandalas out of sand, intricate patterns representing the universe, in order to destroy them with a flick of the wrist when they are finished. I guess Keith is a mandala composed of body parts. After my husband died, a coworker in Stephanies loaned me a book by a Canadian Buddhist nun, which is how I know about mandalas. The nun relates a relatable story about how she was broken open when her husband cheated on her and asked for a divorce. "Thanks, that was beneficial reading material," I told my coworker, but I wished she had entrusted it to me before my husband was eaten alive by his nervous system.

Our warehouse for Keiths isn't so much a warehouse as it is a hospital where all the patients are comatose. The Keiths cry when they are born, but then they are placed into a state of perpetual sleep. Electrodes hooked up to their scalps confirm that their brains emit mostly delta waves. If, by chance, a Keith did dream, would he have anything to dream about, since he has not lived? I imagine Keith's dreams would be like a black vista of space or a blank sheet of paper. Conceptualizing nothingness is difficult. Nonetheless, we take excellent care of the Keiths. Every day, I stretch Keith's limbs, reposition him to prevent bedsores, examine his diaper, cut his toenails and hair should they warrant a trim, lubricate his eyeballs. Of course, we also want the Keiths in prime condition.

Despite the warning not to get attached, I confess that I do have a favorite Keith. My Keith has a small mole beneath his bottom lip, nestled within the indent of his chin, that distinguishes him from the rest. Usually, when a nurse in a Keith

Fulfillment Center acquires a fondness, it's for an infant—a doll of flesh that does not fuss. The veteran nurse among us, Wanda, has reared a Keith from the artificial womb to the operating table. They say she observed while doctors removed his kidneys and corneas. In comparison, my career has been short, a handful of years, but Keith with a mole has been with me the entire time. I worry that he is due imminently, so I secretly strive to provide him extra attention. However, it's important to be cautious; I risk a reprimand, docked pay, for the display of a bias. Cameras were installed after a nurse did something unspeakable to a Nicole she couldn't stand.

I cradle Keith with a mole against my chest to turn him over, then I massage his butt. "You're special," I whisper in his ear, at a moment when I'm pretty sure no one is looking. "You're a special Keith."

The next morning, I am alarmed to discover that Keith with a mole is conscious—or, if not conscious, he is, at least, awake. His stirring occurred during the zombie hours, those two, three, four o'clocks of the graveyard shift, but no one could say exactly when because we dim the lights at night to accommodate circadian rhythms in the skin. I am overcome with guilt, and I remember being made into the bed as a giggling little girl, except now the sheet floating down upon me is horrid complicity. Did I rouse him through the force of my will? "Keiths have occasionally surfaced," the doctors admit. There might be a malfunction in the infusion pump, or his medication wasn't switched. "We'll have him drifting off back into the abyss in a jiffy." The doctors dose Keith with a considerable quantity of barbiturates, yet he does not fall into liminality. "Hmm," they mutter. Keith groans, and though it sounds more like a death rattle, this groan is him rattling to life.

What follows are the tests, the MRIs, the ECTs, the cognitive battery. Exercising the Keiths has limited effect, so he has muscle atrophy, reduction in bone mass, and slackening of the cartilage. He's a violin that has sat unplayed for decades, and he is also constipated. As we attempt to ease him off his nutrient serum with cottage cheese, applesauce, and pureed carrots, he vomits and vomits. It's the instant when Keith with a mole recognizes his reflection that management realizes they have a problem. "Respectfully, we assert that it is ethically tricky to defend cleaning out a Keith who has reached the mirror stage of development," the doctors write in their reports. "Keith," I say as we stare together at his face. "Fief," he replies. "Keith," I repeat, and wiggle his mole. "Teeth," he tries. Keith is better with vowels than consonants. I wonder if I should give him a new name, but that would probably confuse us both.

I'm summoned into the supervision office, and I'm afraid that I'll be fired; instead, they have a proposal. "The Keith Fulfillment Center isn't equipped to handle a walking, talking Keith," they declare. How would I like to become Keith's temporary legal guardian? "You will be compensated," they add. "With the proviso that you agree to restock Keith after we have determined his future." I agree, then I sign forms, a leaning tower of tiny print. From what I can tell, it's a variation on the standard transportation release negotiated with our partner shipping companies. This contract is more voluminous because it accounts for the whole Keith.

"Congratulations," they say. "Please note that the Keith Fulfillment Center is not liable for damages to your health or property caused by a Keith."

We so easily take the basics for granted. As my husband's illness advanced and he lost motor function, digestive function, and, ultimately, mental function, we had to figure them out again. After I got a job in Keiths, I hoped a Keith would allow me to keep my husband with me for longer. In hindsight, that was naïve, since we didn't get to keep our house. A Keith was a precious price to pay for my husband. Most of us are not worth a Keith. I'm overwhelmed by the basics when it comes to Keith with a mole, but I proceed by dressing him in my husband's old clothes. My husband's clothes did not fit him in the end. There was a debate over whether to buy smaller sizes, but we decided, why bother? Now I regret not spending the cash, as his shirts and pants are also loose on Keith. Next, I demonstrate how to go to the bathroom. Sitting on the toilet, I pretend to do my business, then instruct Keith to do the same. Keith sits on the toilet, but he does not pretend to do his business. Is it going to require me taking a shit in front of Keith for him to catch on?

I do not shit in front of Keith, opting to queue videos of mother cats teaching their kittens to use the litter box. He shuffles over to a corner of my living room where there's a desiccated fern, and he defecates. On my shopping list, I scribble in "litter box," which brings me to entertainment. When I guide Keith through the steps of how to watch TV, he wails at cartoons. Cartoons are too bright, too busy, too loud for Keith. Frantically, I navigate back to the kittens. What if Keith happens across something that disturbs him while I'm not here? Should I program parental controls? Even then, Keith could panic if he was unable to click away from a scary puppet reciting the alphabet. Therefore, I indicate to Keith that he must unplug the set if he is frightened. "Off," I explain. "Fob," he answers. His grasp of sequences is strong, regardless of his lag in vocabulary.

Keith is fascinated by true crime documentaries, makeup tutorials, and footage of animals stalking and devouring each other. I lack the desire or the patience to inform him that those animals are extinct and the only species that have endured are those grown for companionship or slaughter. Unlike the aliens in movies who descend to earth and learn to survive among us through television, I don't think Keith absorbs a ton from his shows. He just likes the kissing and murder. Still, I'm concerned that he is bored, or perhaps there is such a surplus of marvels that he appears bored. I'll return to the apartment exhausted by the Keiths, and there is Keith with a mole sprawled across the carpet, huffing on vanilla extract and banging on my pots and pans like they are a set of bongos.

That there is more than one awakening is an epiphany that Keith and I come to accept. There was his physical awakening, then his awakening into his separateness, and, at last, there is his awakening into acknowledging what he is not. Though I had witnessed the relocation of extremely young Keiths into the surgical suite before, they weren't under my care. It can be hard to bear in mind that children are quite as susceptible to disease and ailments as adults. When a toddler Keith of mine is taken, I am surprisingly bereft; I wasn't aware that I had feelings for any Keith besides Keith with a mole. We prepare ourselves emotionally for Keiths to vanish as orders are processed, but you become accustomed to the routine of feeding, washing, touching. In the wing of artificial wombs for Keiths, I was the nurse who attended this toddler's entrance into this world, who listened to his only cry. I cry and cry into the neck of Keith with a mole.

My Keith with a mole wants to console me, and he begins to stroke my stomach, my breasts, but I gesture for him to stop. He is also a child with respect to that matter. Instead, we spoon, and he is happy to be the big spoon. A man in Crystals held me recently after sex, but he aspires to have intercourse with all the nurses in Crystals, Keiths, Stephanies, et cetera. The embrace from Keith with a mole feels like it is for me exclusively. After he has soothed me, he insists in his Keithese on finding out what's wrong. How do I demystify motherhood for someone who doesn't have a mother? My hands clasp my elbows and my arms pantomime a rocking motion, which Keith reflects at me without understanding. So I show him clips of mothers with their human babies. "You?" he asks, in his Keithy way. "No," I say, "I am not your mother."

After his subsequent checkup appointment, I decide to give Keith an impromptu tour of the Keith Fulfillment Center. Doctors and nurses punch him affectionately on the shoulder and encourage him with, "Looking sharp, Keith." It's like we are buddies bonding around the water cooler, except Keith is why we have a water cooler. "This," I say, leading him past the artificial wombs, "is where you were born." When we are in the wing with Keiths around his age, I say, "This is you." As he is the first Keith to view a Keith in the operating theater from a god's perspective, I say, "And this is where Keiths end their term as Keiths."

Wanda is singing in the nursery, even if Keith cannot retain her lullabies. My infant Keith's plastic bassinet, which has been sterilized but not yet reassigned, is startlingly empty. When it catches my eye, it's like seeing someone you think you know who then turns out to be a stranger. I'm keen to gain from Wanda's wisdom, how she avoids overly involving herself with her Keiths. I don't want to trouble Wanda, and chatting about anything not directly Keith-related while on duty is not approved of, so I keep it casual and inquire, "Do you enjoy working in Keiths?" This doesn't have to be awkward, I reassure myself, we are nurses comparing notes. It's not as if I asked what I really wanted to ask, which is how to stop yourself from envying the blissful oblivion of the Keiths. She extends a question to my question while extending this Keith's tendons. "Have you ever dined on a golden egg?" No, I say. "What about the pink beaches at the Coco Palm? Have you paid them a visit?" I had no clue there were pink beaches, I say. Keith can, according to Wanda. Keith can dive beneath the waters and see the famous resorts. We are Keith's family, but he will become a brother, a wife.

When fate closes a door it opens a window, goes the platitude, but in this case Keith is both door and window. He opens the window with his liver. There's a story in the Canadian Buddhist nun's book about a prince who stumbles upon a starving tigress and, in an act of supreme compassion, sacrifices himself to feed her. But in my opinion, the prince should have killed the tigress. She was bound to continue suffering after the prince was gone, until she was gone herself. I have observed myself and my Keiths with a similar sort of compassion, but I can't decide which role is mine. Keith inhabits himself in a parking-lot-during-snow sense that I am incapable of imitating. So he must be the prince and I the tigress. He is not hungering like so many of us to belong in the world. Before Wanda was recruited to the Keith Fulfillment Center, she was employed by a bioremediation service that identified anonymous corpses. If no next of kin or friend or acquaintance claimed the remains, they would be cremated and then stored in a different type of warehouse.

To create a Keith, the lab technician vacates an ovum of its extant tenancy. I contemplate the ova, those microscopic rooms, as Wanda describes searching through the deceased's receipts for products ordered from our warehouses—since the Keith Fulfillment Center is but one branch of a parent company that can also fulfill needs for everything else: area rugs, immersion blenders, socks, half of which will go missing—to confirm a name. Apparently, you come to recognize the deceased's deodorant of choice. A Keith has no accessories other than his body, which is not buried. His donations are treated with the utmost diligence, but the dross of Keith is disposed of like standard medical waste. The warehouse hands joke about unpacking a Keith while they pack up our stuff. They might kid about hazing the newbie by hiding an ear in his lunch, but they are just as subject to scrutiny as we are. And yet they don't have to hassle with a pulse.

The wing of artificial wombs is where nurses tend to spend their breaks. It's called the Aquarium, with the Keiths like fish hovering above us. But the Keiths don't seem much like fish to me, even in their early trimester when they are most liquid. They're closer in aspect to a scented candle than a shark. On one wall there are quaint educational posters of a woman's abdomen, the traditional biological womb. Lately Keith with a mole and I have been transfixed by nature documentaries, and the illustrated female reproductive system, its retinal ovaries sloping into the snout of the womb, resembles the head of a praying mantis. An interesting fact on a poster is that fingerprints are made when the fetus presses up against the mother's uterus. Keith's fingerprints are smooth. His plastic enclosure does not resist—it gives and gives. As I trail Wanda into the wombs, she glows with an embryonic warmth. I am left with the impression that she is a vessel of great sacrifice and purpose.

"Tell me what you felt when your Keith of twenty years was selected," I request.

"Relief," she says. Once a Keith is absent, you remember the tasks you no longer have to do for him, the catheter that can go unchanged. "Embarrassment," she adds. As soon as they opened him, she experienced the same emotion she had as a newly-wed hosting a dinner party, when her mother-in-law pulled up a pair of dirty panties from between the couch cushions.

What did I feel at the death of my husband?

"I felt like I had run errands and forgotten to turn off the oven."

I was convinced the oven would burn down an entire city block.

At the base of an inactive volcano or hunkered in an abandoned nuclear missile silo, there exists a secret Keith Fulfillment Center for elite members. Gossip is that Keiths in the secret center receive pharmaceuticals that are significantly gentler but manufactured at exorbitant cost. Keiths in the warehouses don't have to be perfect—though we do try—provided that they are profitable. But barbiturates are taxing in perpetual doses, so our Keiths often have coronary complications from the medication elevating their blood pressure. They have persistent pneumonia issues or, should they have to depend on those training wheels for oxygenation, fluid in their lungs from ventilators. It doesn't really matter that they're not quite right, as they are universal donor Keiths or Crystals or Jamals, put into production from a consenting original because they can mix and match with the majority of our general members. This secret center, which is also rumored to be outfitted with snipers and hydroponic vegetables, can double as a high-tech survivalist shelter in the event of a revolution by artificial intelligence, or as a respite from the climate refugee crisis and other unpleasant news.

I'm at a loss as to why these high-quality Keiths are hidden from us. The staff wouldn't complain about caring for Premium Keiths—it's not as if the Keiths themselves notice the subtleties between top-of-the-line drugs versus standard sedatives. Yet I've also heard that these pampered Keiths are bespoke Keiths, tailored to suit an individual genome, thus eliminating the original's reliance upon immunosuppressants.

If that is the case, then the Keiths wouldn't qualify as Keiths per se, but as facsimiles of the board, the identical scions of company founders. During happy hour, a nurse in Georges envisions us wheeling in these executives to doze through shareholder meetings while their progenitors are preoccupied. As a result of imagining such an amusing scenario, we come up with a theory for all this clandestine Keithing: our bosses' bosses' bosses and their friends don't want us observing them while they're drooling on themselves. It's of no consequence that the droolers aren't them, if the public can't pick the CEOs from the droolers.

Honestly, caring for drooling CEOs would almost be reassuring, since it would mean that we still have some career security—that no one lives indefinitely, not yet. When scientists in another secret center solve the problem of senescence for our bosses and ensure their immortality, we will be made redundant, but not as redundant as the Keiths. I understand that aging has something to do with the buildup of damage, which sounds a lot like what it's like to grieve, the monotony interrupted briefly for random incidents of frustration and stupidity, such as losing my wedding ring after a visit to the emergency room and finding it later, as a widow, in a bottle of my dead husband's medication. Or it is like submitting another year-end report of my growth and harvest statistics and being told I must increase my target number of dispatched Keiths. Perhaps I would want to live forever if, like it is for the bosses, my participation in work and sickness were optional.

There should be an organ that collects sorrow, that filters it through a pliable labyrinth of lobes or valves, and that isthmus of sadness we could replace, too, when it was worn out, for as Keith has nothing to dream about, he has nothing to mourn. His organ of woe would always stay pink and vital.

The tour was a mistake—too much, too soon. My immediate bosses in the supervision office also don't seem too thrilled with these behind-the-scenes revelations about Keith's distribution. It wouldn't be in the interest of the Keith Fulfillment Center for Keith with a mole to get ideas. "Time to turn in your Keith," they apprise me over the phone. I reply that they cannot have him. Don't fret, they say; they're not harvesting Keith with a mole, they're just going to knock him out with a new cocktail until they have a better plan to integrate rogue Keiths into society. Of course, I persevere in my refusal, but it's irrelevant, as Keith is depressed. He sheds the little weight he's managed to put on since he woke, and he won't depart my bed. "Sleep," he pleads one day. "Sleep with the Keiths." His features are stricken when I laugh, and I feel sorry that Keith isn't sophisticated enough to delight in entendre. What releases me from my commitment to keep him is picturing Keith spending the rest of his life alone and dreamless.

"Don't remember your husband at his weakest, remember him at his strongest" was the unsolicited and offensively sympathetic advice that went around with the flu at my husband's funeral. Recommending that I forget my husband's ill-ness is like saying, "Don't think of an elephant," an elephant that is also a grave. Prior to the notices from collection agencies, then the follow-ups to the notices, then the follow-ups to the follow-ups to the notices, we went to a nice restaurant. A woman was there eating a steak, accompanied by a boy who ran around and screamed. As the boy passed us, my husband interrupted him to ask, "What's your best memory?" My husband assumed, as did I, that this woman was in a crisis she was dealing with as politely as possible. "The necklace!" the boy shouted and resumed screaming. In between screams, the boy had been sucking on a necklace, and when it dropped from his mouth, I couldn't settle on its shape. It was slippery as viscera, umbilical. "He's not mine," the woman said, intuiting our curiosity. Our waiter brought us steaks. "I'm chaperoning him for my sister's ex."

The sister is dead, I later told my husband. You don't know that, he reasoned, the sister could be with her current spouse. We brought my husband's steak home because he wasn't able to finish it, and it rotted. When we moved into our house, I asked him, "How much happiness will we get to have here?" He teased me about it from time to time, saying, "Rate your happiness today on a scale from one to ten." As his illness progressed, he had to rate his pain on a scale from one to ten. I didn't ask about happiness when we moved again. I also didn't ask if pain and happiness were on a continuum, with pain in negative numbers and happiness in positive, or if it diminished both pain and happiness to have them on the same scale. Why the boy in the restaurant was so connected to that necklace I don't know, and naturally I don't know what happened to him after we paid our bill. That's how it is supposed to be with children, even when they're not yours; they outlast their elders, if everything goes right, and their destiny is a mystery. But that doesn't feel right to me—if you create it, you should be there when it is destroyed, to be a palm on the forehead.

Is it fair to impose consciousness on others? My husband and I intended to have children, but what we got was the diagnosis. I dream of Keiths or Stephanies or Daniels or Nicoles we might have made but did not. After my Keith is tucked in and comfortable, I place my palm upon his forehead. Keith was someone in particular once, before he was many and before he was nothing. At least I loved this particular Keith.

"I love you, Keith," I say, and I inject him with a lethal amount of morphine. It was a cache of relief I had apportioned bit by bit for personal use, but, like my husband, like Keith, it was never really mine.

I whisper to my Keith with a mole, "Good night."

the age of love

Walter Perkins was the night nurse on duty who discovered that certain male patients—excuse me, community convalescents—at the North Shore Nursing Home were getting their jollies by dialing up phone sex hotlines. We were both working the graveyard shifts that week and had bonded over the fact that we were the only two guys on the staff, and by making bets on which convalescents listed on the Critical Care board would expire during their sleep. I went to check on a call light, and when I came back his ear was clamped against the receiver in front reception, his dumb ass nearly falling out of the chair from laughing.

"Hey, babe," I said. "What's so funny?"

"You gotta listen to this," he replied, putting the call on speakerphone.

MAN: What do you look like?

OPERATOR: I'm twenty-two years old, with green eyes, D-cup breasts, and long blond hair.

MAN: You sound like my granddaughter. She just entered college to learn how to restore paintings or some malarkey.

OPERATOR: That's nice.

MAN: What kind of getup you got on?

OPERATOR: Oh, not much. Black silk nightgown, thigh-high leather boots, tiny thong.

MAN: Have you been a bad girl?

OPERATOR: So bad.

MAN: You know, when I was young, if we were naughty, what we got was a belt upside the bottom. Do you deserve to be punished?

OPERATOR: I'm getting wet just thinking about it.

MAN: You little tramp. I'm not going to hold back.

OPERATOR: I can't wait, pops. Give it to me.

"Did he say 'malarkey'?" I interrupted.

"Lower your voice," he hissed. Then he added, "It's his third call tonight. Mr. Olson."

"Mr. Olson, I-have-a-pacemaker-and-no-prostate Mr. Olson?"

"The very same. He's been calling adult lines and telling girls he wants to come on their faces. Real hard-core."

"Since when do you listen to the phone conversations of the elderly, sicko?"

"I don't know, since the week the satellite dish was down. It really takes the edge off."

When my shift got out at six, it was and wasn't dark. It was my favorite time of day: driving into the city from the suburbs in advance of dawn, watching joggers huffing and puffing white breath alongside Lake Shore Drive, the ice floes in Lake Michigan rising and falling as if breathing behind them, the Gold Coast cut out crisp and black before it turned gold. I idled down a few blocks looking for a parking spot, then walked to my basement apartment in Andersonville. Grimy light filtered through a single window with iron bars, but it was sufficient. The shower was running as I opened the door. Jill was home.

"I thought I heard you," she said, walking out of the bathroom.

"You're back early," I replied.

"I know. Our last plane never arrived. A blizzard somehow grounded everything in Atlanta. I hopped a commuter from Newark to Detroit to here."

My girlfriend, Jill, worked as a reserve flight attendant out of O'Hare, which meant she had to be ready at any moment if there was an emergency or a regular got the flu. But considering my unconventional care hours, our schedules were complementary.

"Want to join me in the shower?" she asked.

"I have a better idea," I said. "Let's get nasty in the rear of the aircraft."

"I'm tired."

"But you're still in the uniform. Give me the spiel," I coaxed.

"It's amazing to see you again."

"Just humor me."

"Ladies and gentlemen, welcome aboard this Boeing 737 jet with nonstop service to Chicago. Please take a moment to find the exits closest to you, keeping in mind the nearest exit might be behind you." She even threw in the hand gestures.

"We're expecting a bit of a bumpy ride, so keep your seat belt fastened at all times, even when the seat belt sign is not illuminated." Undoing all the buttons on her navy coat, she pulled it off with one swoop, exposing the freckles that topographically traced the slopes of her shoulders.

"Now, before we depart, your tray table should be locked and your seat in its full, upright position. Thank you for your attention, and enjoy the flight." I tugged the stewardess skirt above her hips and bent her over the sofa. Her hair was in a bun, and I unbunned the ensemble while joining the mile-high club here on earth.

Afterward, the two of us lying clean together in bed, I traced a circle with my nose against her damp scalp. Beneath her floral shampoo, I swore I could detect it: the tinny scent of recycled air. It gave me a thrill, almost arousal, from pondering whether she noticed something similar in me, that elephant odor of aged skin. Accustomed to spending such long intervals in enclosed spaces, we both tended to forget how the essence of work lingered with us.

———

It was a couple weeks before I shared another graveyard shift with Wally Perkins, but when I did, he had news. From a gym bag filled with rank tighty-whities and moldy socks, he dug out a clunker tape deck and a bunch of cassettes.

"There's more of them," he said. "They've got a posse. A creepy, cradle-robbing posse of geezers who like to talk about finger-fucking teenage pussy."

"You've been recording this nonsense? You should look into therapy."

"Listen to this one call."

A woman moaning at the peak of pleasure accompanied by ragged breathing scratched through the speakers. Wally rewound and fast-forwarded until he found the right spot.

MAN: Let's pretend I'm a gentleman in my golden years currently killing time in an assisted-living facility, and you are my nurse.

OPERATOR: Assisted living? You mean like an old folks' home?

MAN: Something like that. Your name is Nurse Angela, let's say. You're a hot little number, a feisty Latina. You've got the prettiest brown eyes. You've also got great knockers.

OPERATOR: And what am I wearing? Triangle hat with a red cross on it, white dress with my bust bursting through the buttons, that kind of thing?

MAN: Standard-issue scrubs will do. Pink top and loose pink pants, but bare underneath. Let's also pretend I've got severe arthritis in my joints and lost a foot to diabetes, so I'm confined to a wheelchair.

OPERATOR: Gotcha. So you need me to help with routine tasks, to bend over and lift you in and out of that wheelchair while brushing my big breasts against you, am I right?

MAN: Oh yes. Now, what I want you to do is come into my room and act normal—take my blood sugar, give me my shot, fluff my pillows. Then I want you to shimmy out of those scrubs and sit on my face.

"Wow, so Mr. Harris has a hard-on for Angie," I said. "I can't say I'm surprised. I've seen him chase her around with his stalker eyes."

"I've seen it, too, but to be fair," Wally replied, "I think about me and her in all sorts of compromising scenarios. The only difference is I'm actually in prime physical condition to do something about it."

"Sure, you're such a dreamboat."

"I've been lifting. I'm getting solid pecs."

"So what happens next? She fluffs his pillows, then lets him motorboat her lady pillows, as requested?"

"Pretty much. There's lots of, 'Dios mío, never before have I felt so much pleasure. Your tongue is like el diablo.' Want to hear the rest?"

"As it is now, I don't think I can make eye contact with Angie for a few days."

"Tell me about it. Mr. Klein—you know, the bowlegged guy with the colostomy bag? He's wicked into food. He'll call up girls and be like, 'I am gonna make me an ice-cream sundae on your beautiful body, with macadamia nuts, chocolate syrup, and a cherry on top of your clit.' A few days ago, he told a woman he wanted to eat an open-faced turkey sandwich from her open-faced butt crack. I saw him the following afternoon getting some chicken nuggets in the cafeteria, and I had to look away. He was staring at those chicken nuggets like he was going to do terrible things with them. I can't change his bag anymore without getting the heebie-jeebies."

"Why are you immortalizing this for posterity?"

"Are you kidding? You should get in on it with me. I'm thinking social media, dramatic rights, book deal, the works."

Soon enough, more of the staff found out about Wally's secret project. He would gather anyone who was around for coffee breaks in order to listen to the recent recordings. While he kept trying to convince the rest of us to assist in the taping process, no one took to the idea. Once he managed to set up digital conversions, he privately told me about their online existence in his cloud account. I'd download and queue up one of his audio files in the car during my commute—the hushed voices oddly soothing, like listening to some kind of perverted ocean. On occasion, I would even have them going while cooking a meal or lying on the couch, awash in the nimbus of muted television documentaries on cults.

A virtuoso eventually emerged from among the callers. That was Mr. Rogers, a widower who kept predominantly to himself and who we suspected was the ringleader of the bunch. He was paralyzed on one side due to a stroke a few years prior, and he was all but incontinent. Yet, while he seemed apathetic to physical therapy and regaining his motor skills, he had, apparently through sheer force of will, recovered the clarity and enunciation of his rich speaking voice. We deemed him the best not because he was the freakiest, but because he was in complete command of the conversation from start to finish.

"I bet he got laid like crazy when he could get it up," Wally said one day, after we had listened to a particularly titillating tape.

"Not necessarily," Angie replied. "Sometimes these guys only feel safe getting close to a woman when there's a barrier between him and her."

"Then we shouldn't mention that Mr. Harris has been giving you the most delicious cunnilingus ever, should we?" Wally grinned.

"What? Please say that's not true."

"Oh, it's true. You've been—¡ay caramba!—having the naughtiest time."

"Wonderful. That means you'll have to give him his shots, Walter, since I won't be doing it."

"What is wrong with all of you?" Unbeknownst to us, Chloe, one of the head nurses, had come into the break room. "Don't you realize that our convalescents are human beings who have needs and feelings the same as you? If I hear of any more eavesdropping on their phone calls, disciplinary action will be taken."

"I guess that puts an end to that," I said after she left.

"No way, I'm not stopping," Wally replied. "We'll just have to be more careful."

I spent the rest of my shift assisting wrinkled flesh in and out of bathtubs, irrigating infected bedsores, and spooning mashed potatoes into helpless mouths while in a gloomy funk because of Chloe. When Mrs. Walsh apologized for inadvertently swallowing her glass eye again, I didn't even smile. ("I was trying to give it a clean," the perennial excuse.)

Jill had been around. When I got home, she was sprawled in her underwear on the couch, absorbed in a romance novel.

"How can you stand that trash?" I asked.

"It's just a bit of escapism," she replied. "I pick them up in the airport. What's gotten into you?"

So I told her about the phone sex, Mr. Rogers, and Chloe's reaction. She perked up when I mentioned I had been listening to some of the tapes on my own.

"Does it turn you on?" she asked.

"No, of course not. Don't be silly."

"I'm not being silly. Do you have any with you?"

"Maybe."

"Can you play one for me?"

While I searched for a file on my laptop, she got comfy in a robe and slippers and opened a couple of beers. I queued up "Mr. Rogers Lake Boobies." We sat listening on the couch.

MR. ROGERS: When I was young, we used to go to this beach on the lake. A friend of mine worked as a lifeguard, and we would wait until after hours when it was closed to the public, then go skinny-dipping.

OPERATOR: Sounds sexy.

MR. ROGERS: I want you to imagine we're there now, except instead of summer, it's late fall and chilly. You're my high school sweetheart. It's only us two, and we've snuck under the fence in our coats and boots to brave the water before it freezes.

OPERATOR: Okay, I'm with you. I can feel that harsh autumn wind whipping my cheeks. I blow on my fingers to keep them warm.

MR. ROGERS: Yes, good. I take you by the hand and lead you down to the tide. I can feel you resist with each footstep, but only a little.

OPERATOR: I trust you.

MR. ROGERS: While I remove your coat, you lift my sweater above my arms. I unhook your brassiere and your small breasts pucker.

OPERATOR: God, it's so cold!

MR. ROGERS: You will only have to endure it for a short time. It's not going to last forever. Are you ready?

OPERATOR: I'm ready.

MR. ROGERS: We whoop and scream and sprint into the lake. You feel the shock of waves slapping your shins. The next sensation is constriction, as if you're wearing a garment too tight for your body. After that, panic. We dive. You can feel your heart beat fast, then less fast as it fails to combat the icy temperature. We stay in for thirty seconds, two minutes at most. When we get out, that wind cuts into us. It's almost worse than swimming. You look near tears. We didn't remember to bring a towel.

OPERATOR: I can't feel my toes. Come here. I want your arms around me.

MR. ROGERS: The best I'm able to do is gather our clothes and lead you to the beach house. Maybe there we can dry off before the trip home. It's strung up with Christmas lights that don't work. Inside, it's cleaned out for the season, only a few emergency medical kits lying around. I pull you to me so we stand touching rib cage to rib cage.

OPERATOR: Your touch feels so incredible. I love being pressed against you.

MR. ROGERS: I'm sorry that I brought you here. I thought the water would be just enough of a shock to help you forget for a while.

OPERATOR: Oh well, that's okay.

MR. ROGERS: Your father loved you. He would want you to try to be happy.

OPERATOR: Thanks.

MR. ROGERS: I kiss you. You're trembling. As my lips travel, I taste lake brine mixed with granules of sand. When I enter the warm slickness of your cunt, my skin is still slightly cold. How strange it is to love someone, I think. What are you thinking? What do you feel?

The call went silent. Mr. Rogers was patiently waiting for the operator to answer. I stopped the recording.

"His conversation didn't sound like a fantasy to me," Jill said. "More like a memory."

"It does. The stuff about the dead dad."

"It makes you wonder what's real and what he made up."

"Yeah. They may have gone in the lake, but I doubt he fucked her in that lifeguard house."

"It's actually kind of hot," Jill continued, lowering her tone. "Like, he's got a really sexy voice."

"Oh please."

"He does. Hey, you want to try something?"

"What is it?"

"Talk to me like that," she went on. "Talk to me like Mr. Rogers."

"No. I have to change his diaper tomorrow morning."

"Do it. Say you want to enter the warm slickness of my cunt."

"I want to enter the warm slickness of your cunt."

"No, really get into it. Make your voice sound like his voice."

"I'm sorry, I can't do this. It's too weird."

"Here, I know what we'll do."

She got up, opened another beer, then went into our bedroom and closed the door. In a couple of minutes, my cell phone rang.

"Hey, big boy," Jill said. "Is this better?"

"Not really."

"I'm lying in bed with my legs spread open, thinking of you and touching myself."

"Is that so? Maybe I'll have to make it so you're walking funny down those airplane aisles."

"Give me what I want," Jill replied. "Describe a scene like Mr. Rogers."

"I guess we're at the beach," I began. "It's summer and we've been taking turns cooling off in the water all day. I keep rubbing you down with sunblock and getting really horny." That was terrible. I didn't know why I wasn't able to imagine an original scenario for her, why our phone sex fantasy had to be derived from his fantasy. "Wait. Let me try again. It's summer, and we're at the beach. We've been swimming all day, but around dusk, clouds tumble in. Families pack up coolers, couples leave holding hands, but we stay." Almost unconsciously, I started to see us there, felt my skin raw from sunburn, even found my voice changing to mimic Mr. Rogers's voice like she asked, adopting his deep drawl. "When the droplets hit after sunset, we run to the parking lot, but it's too late. We're caught in the downpour. I search my pockets, but I can't find my keys. I drape you across the hood, and we make love as we're drenched. The aluminum is hot from stored sunlight. The rain becomes warm as it slides down the car." I could hear her breathing faster, insistently.

"Yes," she said. "Now tell me how strange it feels to love someone."

"It feels strange to love you," I said.

She cried out in orgasm. Hanging up, I could hear her through the walls. I didn't go in, though. I didn't feel like I could.

When I braved the bedroom a couple hours later, I found her folded into a fetal ball, asleep. How I wished I could dissolve into a film that lacquered her skin, an invisible armor to safeguard against imminent pains and abrasions. So I crawled under the covers and spooned her. Why did it feel so impossible for me to lie down tenderly with her when she was awake? Growing up, Jill had been an Air Force brat. Her father was a pilot, so Jill, her baby brother, and her mother were alone. He went over to the Middle East; meanwhile, back home, Jill's mom had a string of casual lovers. Apparently the father was willing to ignore the liaisons while he was gone, but even after he returned the mother couldn't break her habit. Jill had hardly seen him: the occasional phone call, the occasional lunch. Her brother, too, enlisted in the Air Force and now flies drones in the skies above Afghanistan.

From Los Angeles, New York, Miami, and Detroit, from Denver, Seattle, and D.C., Jill wanted to talk dirty. "Whisper the latest sweet nothings of Mr. Rogers in my ear," she'd say. Once, she stopped by the home late at night on her way from the airport. She marched in bright and chipper with her roller bag as if she hadn't been working constantly for the past week.

"Where is he?" she asked. "Can we spy on him?"

Reluctantly, I agreed, hoping he would become not so intriguing. We took the elevator up to the Butternut Wing (each wing was named after a different kind of squash) and tiptoed past Mr. Rogers's quarters. He had dozed off to a novel, reading glasses nearly tipping off the cliff of his nose. Jill watched him for a couple minutes, then left without saying another word.

Around the time she visited, a newly admitted convalescent, Mr. Sullivan, also joined the phone sex squad. He was special in that we couldn't find his conversations amusing or exciting, merely pitiful.

OPERATOR: I jump in topless and giggling into the hot tub. I can't wait to get my hands on your giant erection hiding under the bubbles.

MR. SULLIVAN: Can I call you Anne?

OPERATOR: You can call me whatever you want.

MR. SULLIVAN: My wife's name was Anne.

OPERATOR: Anne is a pretty name.

MR. SULLIVAN: I shouldn't say "was." She's alive, but in hospice care at my daughter's house.

OPERATOR: I'm sorry.

MR. SULLIVAN: She and her husband didn't feel they could take care of us both once her mother was diagnosed as terminal. I'm in a geriatric facility until there's a better plan.

OPERATOR: How awful.

MR. SULLIVAN: I'm worried they'll forget I'm here once my wife dies. Sometimes I want her to hurry up and die so I can get out of this place. It's one thing to imagine where you'll end your days, another thing to know. That bed, this chair.

"I can't keep listening to him," Angie said. "It makes me sad."

"I'm curious what kind of people dial phone sex hotlines nowadays, in the age of internet porn," Wally said. "Is it just a bunch of grandpas who never got comfortable using a computer?"

"No idea," Angie replied. "Maybe it's nice to have somebody who's participating with you."

"What do you think our generation will be like when we get to that stage? Will dirty old men be jerking off to money-shot montages instead of calling up asking women to behave like nymphomaniac nurses? These are questions of our times."

I had read a photo caption about eldercare strategies tested around the country. One of them involved giving every resident a plushie unicorn they could cuddle and that would make vague horsey noises of delight. More than a few of the men and women bonded so intensely with their unicorns that they opened up to them as they never did with the staff or even their friends among the residents. The researchers knew this, since there was a microphone hidden beneath the red tongue of each placid unicorn. They hypothesized that people in that late stage of life found it safer to reveal their deepest selves to an object, as it would never abandon them, never judge. Perhaps, they reasoned, the elderly would feel safer being attended by machines. I related this anecdote to my coworkers.

"That's great," Wally replied. "I can't wait to walk in on Mr. Sullivan telling Sparkles that he's crying because he never got the proper opportunity to say farewell to his wife."

"You won't be there at all," Angie said.

Then, out of the blue, the members of the phone sex clique started to croak. The first was Mr. Olson, the sadist. The coroner ruled he had suffered a massive myocardial infarction. We found him slumped over in bed, pajamas only half on, the bulk of his pacemaker useless inside his chest. The next to go was Mr. Klein, the foodie. The cancer in his bowels grew back, and he was transferred for treatment. Wally still cracked jokes at his expense, supposing the poor guy was calling the hotlines from Northwestern Memorial, telling girls he wanted to eat his fruit cups and Tater Tots off their tits. Mr. Harris, the diabetic with the nurse fetish, was stable but hadn't placed an outgoing call in forever. We guessed this reticence was caused by Angie getting other nurses to cover his room. That left only Mr. Sullivan and Mr. Rogers, and our incontinent Casanova had also seemingly gone silent. Wally hadn't played me any of his conversations, and Jill had stopped asking questions. She'd become more aloof in general—calling less when she was away, not in the mood for sex when she was home. So when I saw the light to Mr. Rogers's phone go on when I was manning front reception on my own, I picked up to listen. Jill was in San Francisco; I had just said good night to her on my cell. I felt an unwelcome wave of déjà vu upon immediately hearing her voice. Of course, this was followed by the recognition that it wasn't a surprise.

JILL: I don't think he suspects. Besides, it's not like I'm doing anything wrong. I haven't cheated on him.

MR. ROGERS: What is it that you love about him?

JILL: I'm not actually sure. I think I fell in love with his hands. I thought it was nice when he told me that he took care of old people for a living. I liked imagining his hands at work, attending to needs. There was something kind about their clean nails. It feels like there's something missing in our relationship, though. He doesn't really want to delve into emotional stuff. I know his father bailed on his mom after she was diagnosed with ALS. They managed on their own for a few years until her condition forced them to hire a live-in nurse. We really don't have to go into all that. What do you want to talk about tonight?

MR. ROGERS: I've been thinking a lot about a girl I used to know. One summer, I worked in the kitchen of a hotel in Maine, mostly washing dishes and drinking with the chefs.

The family who owned the hotel also owned one of those corporate coffee brands. Their daughter was there on vacation from Radcliffe, and we got to know each other.

JILL: Good for you—a fling with the boss's daughter.

MR. ROGERS: It wasn't erotically intimate, but we spent a lot of time together. I want you to put yourself in her shoes, to talk to me like she did, to tell me your secrets.

JILL: What do I say? I'm going to need a little more information.

MR. ROGERS: Don't worry too much about the particulars. Do you have any alcohol?

JILL: There's some in the minibar.

MR. ROGERS: Pour yourself a glass. She had keys to the whole place, and we'd steal bottles from the wine cellar.

JILL: Okay, I've got some.

MR. ROGERS: So start talking, Jill. Imagine I'm with you as we sit in a humid and empty kitchen.

JILL: Well, my father wasn't around much. My mother was sleeping with some men. There were always a couple unfamiliar faces in the house. I remember I got home from school one afternoon, and when I went upstairs my mom was riding this guy with the bedroom door wide open, and as she saw me there watching in the hallway, she paused, smiled, and waved, then started back up.

MR. ROGERS: Did she talk to you about it?

JILL: No, she didn't. But she often said it was healthy for children to know their parents are sexual beings.

MR. ROGERS: I'd like to kiss you.

JILL: You mean over the phone?

MR. ROGERS: Yes, over the phone.

JILL: I think I'd like to kiss you.

MR. ROGERS: I lean in and part your mouth with mine. Your lips taste—

I hung up. I ran upstairs to the Butternut Wing. Mr. Rogers's room was locked, but I searched through my set of keys until I found a match. When I crashed in, he was not on the phone with Jill. He was sitting smug, staring down the door.

"What do you think you're doing, talking to my girlfriend?"

"She's the one who calls me."

"I bet the phone sex girls pay you to talk to them, too."

"Well, it's clear you're doing a great job meeting her needs as a lover."

"You think you can do better from that wheelchair?"

"Kid, you clearly haven't the foggiest notion of what women want."

"Don't talk to Jill again, or I will make you regret it."

"I shit my pants about five minutes ago. I'm going to need a change."

Mr. Rogers was an anus. Mr. Rogers needed to die. I imagined smothering him with his favorite blankie or tipping his wheelchair down a flight of stairs or bludgeoning him to death with the phone in his room. It's a beautiful day in the neighborhood, bitch. Instead, I left him there, marinating in his own feces. There were several texts and missed calls from Jill on my cell, but I ignored them. In my head, I kept replaying both her and my conversations with him the rest of the night, as I drove home at dawn, and into the next day. How could he dismiss me so easily?

When Jill walked in the door that evening, she immediately started apologizing. Wally had suggested that the two of them surprise me with the tapes. The whole thing was meant to be a joke. She was planning on telling me before it went too far, but then she got to like the guy.

"I don't want you to talk to Mr. Rogers ever again," I said.

"I can't do that," she replied. "I care."

"Then you're not sorry."

"I'm sorry for hiding it from you. I'm not sorry for calling him."

"Don't you get it, Jill? He's using you. This isn't a real relationship. You don't know him. How can you trust what he says?"

"I trust him," she said. Jill came over and sat next to me. She slid an arm around my shoulders. "Have you ever thought that maybe he's just lonely?"

I tried to kiss her with all the feeling she said she was missing. I wanted affection that felt true and unrehearsed, an urgent kind of love. "Whoa, slow down," Jill said. "Can Mr. Rogers do this to you?" I asked, rubbing my erection against her thigh. "Nope," she said. "He can't." She stood up from the couch. "I don't want you when you're desperate."

Walter Perkins was fired after Mr. Sullivan committed suicide. His wife was still alive, still in hospice at his daughter's house, so we figured his depression wasn't out of the ordinary. He had written a note before sneaking out his first-story window—completely in the nude—to die of exposure in the snow. "Tell Anne I'm going on a new adventure!" it read. Somehow, he had rigged the alarm around his ankle not to sound upon his escape. An investigation was conducted into why the staff had failed to prevent the death. After Chloe learned that Wally had continued to make tapes, it didn't matter that he hadn't been on duty when it happened; he was told to collect his things. Right before walking out, he bequeathed to me his recorder.

"I don't need it anymore," he said.

"I can't exactly say I feel sorry for you, Wally," I replied.

"Anyway, I've got to get out of here. I'm going to apply to work in construction. A job where I can get ripped. I want to be the guy girls think about when they touch themselves before they go to sleep."

"Best of luck with that."

A week later, Angie and I shared the graveyard shift. She and I weren't chitchatters, but that night she came and sat next to me with her coffee.

"Chloe called me out on avoiding Mr. Harris," she said.

"Oh, who cares?" I said.

"I've felt guilty about it ever since Mr. Sullivan died, yet I can't make myself go in that room."

"It's just a fantasy," I said. "It doesn't mean anything."

"Even if that's true, I wouldn't know the first thing to say to him anymore."

"So tell Chloe he was sexually harassing you, and she'll assign me or one of the other nurses to him from now on. She won't give you crap about it. Problem solved."

"But he didn't sexually harass me. He had a private fantasy that he thought he had kept private. I wish I had never listened to the tapes."

As Angie left, I saw the light go on indicating Mr. Rogers was on the phone in his room. I hooked up Wally's device, clandestinely picked up the receiver, and hit record.

The next day, I tried to fulfill my promise. I went to Chloe and informed her that Mr. Rogers had lashed out, hitting me around the face and shoulders that morning while I dressed him in a fresh diaper and pair of pants. "He didn't do much damage, because he's very weak," I said. "Unfortunately, this isn't the first time he's acted abusively like this, and I'm worried it's becoming a habit." Chloe offered me her most medical scowl in response. "That is unfortunate," she sighed. "He's been such a model resident until now, so calm and polite. Has anyone else reported this kind of behavior? They can get funny, our elderly, about particular staff members for no discernible reason. I can see to it that he's usually covered by a different nurse." I told her that Mr. Rogers had been the mastermind behind the phone sex ring, and he had also egged on Mr. Harris to harass Angie, who felt bad for him and didn't want to formally complain. Wasn't aggressiveness and lack of inhibition a side effect for a man in his condition?

"Indulging in sexual fantasies is not a side effect of stroke," Chloe replied. "But that is serious. I promise my handling of this will be a priority."

"What does that mean?" I asked.

"There's an entire procedure we have to follow by law before transferring problem residents to a more rigorous facility," she explained. "I'll start by contacting his family."

I felt satisfied that the future that lay in wait for Mr. Rogers involved him getting punted to some nightmare prison for the senescent where he would be handcuffed to a bed for the rest of his days; thus I had won. But when I came home after my shift, I found Jill packing for one of her trips, and she didn't acknowledge my existence.

"Where to this time?" I asked.

"It's an international flight," she said, "London Heathrow,

then on to Berlin. I'll be in first class. Somebody called in last minute with food poisoning."

"That's fancy," I said. "Have fun." I went to kiss her, but she turned away to zip up her roller bag.

"I wanted to let you know that I'm not going to live here when I get back," she replied. "I'll come by when you're at work and get my things. You won't have to see me."

"Are you breaking up with me?"

"Did you honestly believe I wouldn't find out? He has my cell phone number. Apparently someone reported him as a 'disruptive influence in their senior community.' I think that's how it was phrased. The head nurse called his stepdaughter, who adores him. He paid for her education and her wedding and adopted her and everything."

"So this is about Mr. Rogers? I wasn't the one who reported him. I mentioned repeatedly that he was dangerous."

"I told him he has my consent to disclose the nature of our relationship to your boss, so we'll see what happens," Jill replied. "You're not a good person." She buttoned up her coat and adjusted her navy hat.

"Jill, wait," I said. "Let's talk about this."

"I don't have time," she said.

I watched the icicles melt from our barred window and imagined Jill commuting to the airport. In a couple of hours, she would be thirty thousand feet above the earth and breathing the same air as three hundred strangers. The illuminated nerve centers of our human cities would pulse below as the plane winged its way toward a refreshingly light continent, free of her memories. She had told me she missed being in flight, so I bought her a white noise machine. However, it quickly ended up in the storage closet. It couldn't simulate the feeling of distance, of being confined in a space with no one you were required to know. I could see her distributing pillows and blankets. I could see her offering beverages to passengers passing the time in their seats. I could hear her voice collectively soothing them over the intercom. When she finally exited the aircraft, the mouths would speak a language she could not understand. Maybe when she deplaned a plane in another country she could pretend she was an entirely different person.

I had saved Mr. Rogers and Jill's last conversation. I found it and turned the speakers on our stereo up as loud as they reached.

JILL: I think I'm at the point where I want to leave him, but I'm afraid.

MR. ROGERS: Why are you afraid?

JILL: I'm afraid I won't find anyone better. I don't want to be alone. What was it like when you lost your wife?

MR. ROGERS: I didn't know what to do with myself at first. But I didn't love my wife any more or any less than the women before her. In the end, of course, everyone either leaves you or you leave them. Everyone is afraid of old age, but it's not so terrible. If you've been lucky enough not to let misery get the best of you, old age can be the age of love.

JILL: What if I never find someone to love me again?

MR. ROGERS: Don't worry. You have your whole life ahead of you to love someone. You are so young. You are so beautiful.

frequently asked questions
about your craniotomy

I f you're reading this page, chances are you've recently heard that you need to have a craniotomy. Try not to worry. Although, yes, this is brain surgery, you're more likely to die from the underlying condition itself, such as a malignant tumor or subdural hematoma. Think of it this way: insomuch as being alive is safe, which it is not, having a craniotomy is safe. We fill our days with doing laundry, replacing our brake pads at the auto shop, or making a teeth-cleaning appointment with the dentist, in the expectation that everything will be fine. But it won't. There will be a day that kills you or someone you love. Such a perspective is actually quite comforting. Taken in that light, a craniotomy can be a relaxing experience, rather than one of abject terror.

WHAT HAPPENS DURING A CRANIOTOMY?

Nearly all operations begin with the creation of a bone flap so the doctor has an opening into your brain. This opening will be sealed shut at the end with wire or titanium plates and screws. Beneath the bone are the three meninges, connective membranes also known as the mothers: the *dura mater* (hard mother), *arachnoid mater* (spidery mother), and *pia mater* (soft mother). After we're past that triple embrace—like the Moirai crones of myth that spin, measure, and cut the thread of life—we're at the precious substance of thought. The blush of living brain has been described as resembling the inside of a conch shell or a crumbling marble quarry. To me, it's like the revelation of brine and meat after shucking an oyster. Beyond that, what happens during a craniotomy depends on the type of surgery. A translabyrinthine craniotomy, for example, involves cutting away the whole of the mastoid bone and some of the tunnels of your inner ear.

IS IT TRUE I WILL HAVE TO BE AWAKE DURING MY CRANIOTOMY?

Some craniotomies require you to be conscious. When a tumor makes itself comfortable with a good book and a blanket in front of the fire of your eloquent cortex, which controls language or motor functions, we give you prompts indistinguishable from online banking security questions. Certain surgeons fancy themselves as early explorers, sketching out crude cartographies of the thunderous Badlands, the twists of the Amazon, the jagged coasts of Jutland brainscapes. I like to think of the organ as an ancient manor or primordial motel and myself a plumber, electrician, or stonemason reading a blueprint of where to find the stairways, hidden chambers, fuse boxes, boiler, septic tank. It's a Versailles of the id and ego with a fleshy, well-manicured hedge maze.

WON'T I BE IN PAIN IF I'M AWAKE DURING MY CRANIOTOMY?

You will be awake for a short interval during the craniotomy. Also, there are no pain receptors in the brain. What you might undergo are moments of aphasia or synesthesia, like Kandinsky hearing his paint box hiss or Schubert visualizing E minor as "a maiden robed in white with a rose-red bow on her chest" when he heard chords struck in that key. The hallucinations aren't as enchanting. You think you have it bad enough getting brain surgery, then suddenly the OR is covered in roaches. A woman once met her long-lost twin. She didn't have a long-lost twin. There was also the estate lawyer who decided that his entire surgical team was trying to kill him and wouldn't stop screaming, "You'll never make me talk!" Reports of out-of-body experiences aren't uncommon. I've heard it feels as though you are watching your own handwriting uncoiling from someone else's pen.

WHAT WILL MY BRAIN BE LIKE AFTER MY CRANIOTOMY?

It will go on with its braining, provided we got all the cancer or your growth was benign. If you have a tumor that has seeded itself throughout your cerebrum like an aspen grove, however, or been diagnosed with a glioblastoma multiforme, you will have a different kind of recovery.

In such circumstances, your craniotomy will be followed by radiation. We might even implant some wafers in your head and light you up like a plug-in bust of Christ. Patients tend to squeeze out at most another year after this; vigorous or younger individuals can last a smidge longer. What occurs next is this: fatigue, mood swings, muscle weakness, confusion as to the purpose of a toaster. Family and friends drop by to tell you that you're an "inspiration" or to utter phrases about "the indomitable human spirit." There's the wearing of wristbands and ribbons and the guilt donation of a dollar to the Leukemia & Lymphoma Society or other cancer research organizations at the grocery store or pharmacy. Positive social media updates about your progress or how the tumor "may have killed a couple of brain cells but can't kill your sense of humor" will proliferate. Chemo makes you lose weight.

Steroids make you gain weight. You spend hours on internet medical forums, lament the hours spent on internet medical forums, then spend more hours on internet medical forums. You vow to quit the internet altogether and immediately spend more hours on internet medical forums.

Later: Constant nausea isn't relieved by medication because it's caused by cranial swelling. Thrush invades your esophageal tract like you're a neglected fourth-grade science project. Incontinence, memory loss, the inability to wield utensils. Epiphanic moments and inexplicably beautiful solitary hours are devoured by rage. The joy of sunlight, the decency in rain; the hatred of sunlight, the disgust at rain. Your long-suffering, Florence Nightingale spouse grows distant. Neighbors avoid your house in fear they will have to engage in small talk with you or your family. There's discussion of Kübler-Ross's Stages of Grief and where you might be—when in doubt, choose "Bargaining." Manically, you sort through storage boxes in your attic or basement and, also manically, sort through memories. Diets, tonics, acupuncture sessions, and other alternative holistic methods are tried. You ingest so much flaxseed, but flaxseed can't cure everything.

Much later: Pain pills are increased to straight-up morphine to, finally, liquid morphine that's absorbed inside the cheek because you're too tired to sit up or even swallow. Hospice workers visit who seem like they've been sent straight from the choirs of seraphim; hospice workers visit who you want to punch in the face because they talk about "wanting to give back" or "observing the whole range of the human condition." Your spouse or mother or child caretaker is overwhelmed by a crying jag at the sight of a newly delivered commode chair. Your spouse or mother or child caretaker gives you a haircut and you feel fully afraid and not just numbly afraid as you watch your thin hair on the floor get swept away. Your spouse or mother or child caretaker, if artistically inclined, draws your likeness while you nap. This likeness won't be completed and is left, parchment edges curling, with only one wide turtle eye. Plan on being brought outside for a last trip to see the migration of geese. A dry fever calms you and shuts down all your bodily systems. You breathe harder and harder until you stop.

A few families have even claimed that reckoning with a fatal diagnosis strengthened their bond. I'm here to tell you that dealing with the brain and its illnesses is comparatively simple. It merely requires a good mechanic. What's trickier to work with is the mind. There are symptoms that cannot necessarily be mitigated with hospice care or a prescription, such as when your spouse informs you that, even though you are a brain surgeon, he is too depressed to leave the house and pick up the boys at school or walk the dog. Perhaps you're not as understanding as you should be, seeing as marriage to a female brain surgeon is like winning the devotion of a unicorn. Instead of him telling you that he won't be able to attend the parent-teacher conference, you should be telling him that you won't be able to attend the parent-teacher conference. You should not be the one to clean up golden retriever feces off the kitchen floor.

WHAT ARE THE COMPLICATIONS THAT CAN OCCUR FROM A CRANIOTOMY?

Ability to understand language but not to speak. Ability to speak but not understand language. You might become the relative who throws the turkey at holiday dinners. At least it's not as bad as trephination. Doctors in the Dark Ages used to create burr holes to relieve pressure or remove mental illness, meaning you'd have a permanent open wound in your head, but when they were done, they let patients keep the round piece of bone. Men and women wore the bone around their necks as a charm to ward off evil spirits. I bet it also came in useful for scaring the hell out of one's nephews.

The worst complication I know of is when an ENT stuck a probe up a patient's nose and punctured the blood-brain barrier because it was unusually low. Each time the patient took a breath, oxygen siphoned into his cranium and couldn't escape until he herniated his brain into the vertebral canal. There lurk beastlier medical boogeymen, such as super-gonorrhea or the strain of MRSA resistant to known antibiotics. Eventually, you may not be able to get a rhinoplasty for fear of dying from a staph infection.

If that was blunt, that is because I have been dulled. Today,

I had an emergency surgery on a senator for an arteriovenous malformation (a congenital tangle of blood vessels—a Gordian knot of gray matter) who could shut us down based on his demands for Medicare cuts, then got dragged to the emergency room for a thoracic burst fracture, and meanwhile I'm buzzed nonstop with requests for consults. I'm also forced to fetch my own fresh frozen plasma. On top of it all, I drew the short straw to write this FAQ page for our website because, our director said, we want it to have that personal touch. Now that I am single, I'm also the sole guardian at home (or not at home) responsible for getting a couple of adolescent boys who are both flunking math to stop watching porn or playing video games and do their homework. My apologies if my bedside manner comes across more Groucho Marx than Mother Teresa.

WHY SHOULD I CHOOSE ST. TERESA OF ÁVILA HOSPITAL FOR MY CRANIOTOMY?

The Department of Neurological Surgery at St. Teresa's has been recognized for decades as one of the foremost specialty centers that focuses on the brain and spinal cord. Surgeons from all over the globe come to learn about the latest minimally invasive—and the latest maximally invasive—techniques. It's deliberate that Saint Teresa of Ávila happens to be the patron saint for headache sufferers. Tales from hagiographies describe her mystical trances wherein she would feel herself be stabbed through the heart and out her intestines with the fiery golden lance of God, causing excruciating spiritual torment. Hospital halls are built for suffering. Teresa's mantra was, "Lord, let me suffer or let me die."

CAN YOU TELL ME ABOUT YOUR SURGICAL TEAM?

Though I wouldn't necessarily call us a team, I did fill in as pitcher so the hospital could participate in league softball playoffs. Dr. Jay Katz couldn't make it because he had a Whipple. Jay is a terror both on and off the mound. He can remove half a patient's pancreas without having to pee. I'd have to rig myself up with a catheter. Dr. Amy Benson is our go-to skull-base surgeon. She recently returned from maternity leave. Now the only thing we hear about is the coltish softness of fontanels, the magical myelination moment of development when her baby recognized—I mean really recognized—her face. Maybe I'm just jealous she has a child who recognizes her face. Dr. Chen, our primary pediatric specialist, decided to retrain from dermatology after his son died of an astrocytoma. I'm very sorry Dr. Chen's son died of an astrocytoma, and I'm sorry that we're compared to the example of heartbroken-but-nonetheless-resilient goodness set by Dr. Chen. Then there is Dr. Steve Stevens, who has a decent name for a nemesis; he is the director of neurosurgical operating rooms at St. Teresa of Ávila and once left a sponge behind in a patient's brain. Do not permit a man with essentially the same first and last name to operate on your spine, his forte, the most lucrative specialization in our field.

As for me, I have a totaled Lexus, the academically indifferent sons, an acute condition of plantar fasciitis, a touch of alcoholism, and the no-longer-toilet-trained golden retriever. But you don't really want to know this, do you? It's like when you were a kid and you ran into your teacher parting the mist on some veggies in the grocery store and it dawned on you, "Wow, Mr. Wilson must have to move through linear time."

YOU'RE KIND OF ANGRY, AND THAT'S NOT VERY PROFESSIONAL. IS EVERYTHING OKAY?

I feel betrayed by the brain. The brain is more or less the same in everyone; there is the Broca's area, that cul-de-sac of speech in the arcuate fasciculus, and there is the hippocampus, that seahorse of memory, nestled in the temporal lobe. But when you think of the color red, do you picture the insistent primal red of an emergency vehicle or the deep burgundy of an aged wine? If I asked you to visualize a chair, would you picture an ornately carved dining chair or a plush recliner? Similarly, I thought my husband was predictable; I knew which entrée he would order at restaurants, which jokes would elicit a laugh. Then I found my husband in the garage after his suicide by gunshot to the head, and our relationship no longer made sense. I assumed I had known the locations and boundaries of things, where he tended to take off his shoes, the weekend afternoons he liked to be left alone. The older brother he used to idolize had overdosed. My husband was sad, and after a while I became exasperated with him, because I assumed that I understood where the edges of that sadness were. Now I wonder: When I am resecting a brain to prevent seizures, for example, what am I even attempting to fix?

HAVE YOU EVER THOUGHT ABOUT NOT BEING A NEUROSURGEON?

It's absurd that I apprenticed and studied for my entire youth to help others live longer so that they can continue to melt the polar ice caps while enjoying party subs. Still, I am rather fond of my rongeurs, my retractors. After a while, everything becomes routine. My favorite part is when we're offered up sheep corpses to test prototype drill bits.

Unless you're Saint Teresa and have taken holy orders, you feel the despair of the clinician, particularly when working with children. Suturing peach fuzz or reopening a bone flap to drain the cerebrospinal sap of a girl with brain swelling leaves a bittersweet existential aftertaste. I sobbed in a supply closet, the first real, gulping sob since I was an intern, after I accidentally nicked the sinus of a toddler with epilepsy and saw the blood drenching my scrubs down to my shoe covers. "I'm trapped," I remember muttering, and not merely because I was huddling in a locked supply closet. There's a dissociation from yourself, similar to what patients report feeling upon that first tug of anesthesia. When I was removing a pituitary recently, I had the thought, What if I abandoned my sons and simply worked at the food court in an airport?

HOW ARE YOU GOING TO MOVE ON WITH YOUR LIFE?

After I took out that pituitary, I found myself driving to the mall. Both of my sons had after-school vandalism and weren't going to be home until late. Escalators that were past the point of caring about anything, a feeling I identified with, stitched me up several floors in a department store until I arrived in the blissful sauna of fabrics that was the section for evening gowns. An emerald-green dress covered in sequins with a plunging neckline was the first to flash to my brittle attention, and I looped it over an arm raw from surgical soap. In the changing room, as I was determining, "My boobs probably cannot handle this," a female voice, perfectly pitched in helpfulness, had to inquire, "How are you doing in there?" When I opened the door, she fluttered into an excited clap and said, "It looks so great on you! Really brings out the color of your eyes." I told her my eyes are brown. "Of course," she recovered immediately, "but I can see ocher, almost amber flecks in them when you're wearing that dress." Did I want her to gather up some others that I might like better? She resembled my mother, who had raised me by herself and been so proud of my reliable profession and my reliable husband, who had worked odd jobs to support us—she had been a waitress and a secretary and a stockist of blue jeans—but forty years younger, reincarnated and karmically forced to work retail for eternity. Though maybe that was my dumb imagination too sentimental from bereavement.

The twenty-something reincarnation of my mother brought me a strapless golden dress of stiff satin that curved like a bell but with a slice cut out of it at the front, as if my legs were the clapper on display. "Absolutely not," I said. She brought me a dress that was layers of frothy raspberry tulle. "I'm the human embodiment of a smoothie." She brought me a duchesse-silk bustier dress that was hand-beaded with pearls and lacy corsages that looked like crumpled baby fists. "They don't look like the hands of ghost babies to you?" She brought me a classic black sheath dress with a slinky train that shimmered royal neon blue, so it felt as though I were nearly constantly tripping on an electric eel. "Is this for a special occasion?" she asked. Such information might give her a clearer idea of the best ensemble for my needs. "It's for the Medulloblastoma Ball," I replied. "Is that a new start-up?" A variety of brain tumor, I explained. There was no Medulloblastoma

Ball; I had invented it on the spot, and the fake event conjured pictures of globular brain tumors in formal wear awkwardly holding each other at the waists during a slow dance in a junior high gymnasium.

"I hope you don't personally know anyone affected," my retail mom said, with that concerned-from-a-mountaintop look surgeons use when they're giving bad news but they don't want to hug. "My husband died from a medulloblastoma," I lied, and she came down the mountain in what appeared to be genuine sympathy. She must have realized she was going to have to hug. "My intuition homed in on a sad aura around you," she whispered into my hair while hugging me. "I am sad," I agreed and became preoccupied with the thought that she might spot errant gristle nestled in my bun. Despite the most herculean of hygienic efforts, it's funny where you'll find tissue—your hair, the corner of your lips, in your bra. "When did you last make the space for self-care?" she pressed on. "I can't mourn my dead husband with pedicures or spa treatments," I protested. No, no, that's not what she meant, but she could let me in on her secret if I was interested. Her secret, she continued without waiting to find out if I was interested, was to take one ordinary action—pouring a glass of water, or peeling an orange—and slow it down, slow it way down until it becomes almost unbearably beautiful, then recite to herself, "I am alive." It's a trick of your nervous system that speeds along the process of allowing psychic wounds to heal. In response I said something like, "I guess I am going to buy the sparkly green dress that brings out all the not-green in my eyes for the totally legitimate brain cancer dance."

DID YOU TAKE THE ADVICE OF THE DEPARTMENT STORE REINCARNATION OF YOUR MOTHER?

I wore that emerald gown out of the store, and I was wearing it when I bought a case of cheap sauvignon blanc, setting the alcohol on top of my balled-up scrubs in the passenger seat, and when I got home, I wore the emerald gown as I uncorked a bottle and slowly, ever so slowly, poured the liquid into a glass and took a sip. Conclusion: I felt the same amount of boring PTSD. Operating in the emerald gown would be so glamorous, I mused, provided I had matching hairnet and face mask accessories also studded with emeralds. Wouldn't it be fun to cut into a brain, adorn it with gems, and then cover that diadem back up with the patient's skull? A surgeon could remove a tumor but replace it with a sapphire or ruby. The emerald gown and I let the golden retriever out to take a shit in the middle of the driveway, then the golden retriever, the gown, and I lay in bed, where I drank the rest of the opened wine. Since my husband killed himself, the golden retriever sleeps on his side while the dog bed on the floor remains empty and disgusting. That dog bed has probably been disgusting for a while, but only now that the dog no longer uses it do I find the dog bed beyond repulsive.

My sons returned and yelled for me. "I'm in the bedroom," I yelled back at them, and they located me in the bedroom. "What do you think of my new dress?" I asked. They were standing extremely still, too still for teenage boys, which meant they were either afraid that they would be told to do something or afraid of something I would do. "I hate it," the elder son unambiguously passed judgment. "Yeah, it's ugly," the younger confirmed. "You're right. It is hideous," I said, rolling the depleted wine bottle against my leg and listening to the sequins ting. "What should we do with it?" "Run over it with the lawn mower," Elder proposed. "Throw it in the pool!" exclaimed Younger. "To the pool!" I decreed, stripping off the dress, at which they made gagging sounds and averted their gazes, then I slowly, ever so slowly, just to mess with them, donned a robe also slept on by the dog. That time I felt an increase in tranquility, so my retail mother's advice did work. "Goodbye, you worthless overpriced knockoff dress I spent money on for no reason!" I shrieked as I hurled the dress into the pool. The dress pirouetted elegantly in the jets like a jellyfish or a severed mermaid tail. Water was the proper medium for dresses, I decided. Celebrities at the Met Gala should promenade down the red carpet and into an enormous fish tank. "Toss whatever you want into the pool," I told my sons. Were there exceptions, rules, items that if lost to the depths would later make me mad? "Do your worst," I said, then added, "as long as it won't electrocute us."

WHAT ELSE DID YOUR FAMILY THROW IN THE POOL?

A nine-iron, a leftover jar of marinara sauce, medical text-books, my son's calculus textbook, which I remembered he is failing, my other son's history textbook, which he also is probably failing, my dead husband's button-down shirts, a couple of pork chops. Our filter buckets are often clogged with snakes, frogs, and tiny lizards—a chlorinated witch's cauldron—so a pork chop, I reckoned, with its plush padding of fat, could make a welcome life raft for some desperate gecko. In went a hammer, a basketball, and a single leather glove, as though we had challenged the pool to a duel. A Nativity set was sacrificed, and drowned, too, were child-hood action figures, those superheroes and supersoldiers, intriguing me as to what they might bring as gifts to round out the frankincense and myrrh. Additional flotation devices for the geckos in the form of couch cushions were hurled, and under them I made a note to check for untold quarter, booger, and, most important, benzodiazepine treasures. The gross dog bed was chucked, so for good measure I pushed in the dog. We laughed at him as he paddled around the obstacle course of our crap in that terribly inconvenienced yet gentlemanly manner of swimming dogs. When the boys carried out the framed photo of the four of us from the foyer with their father's arms around each of them, I said, "Okay, stop now, that's enough."

IS THERE A PIECE OF HOPE YOU CAN IMPART TO READERS OF
THESE FREQUENTLY ASKED QUESTIONS, SOMETHING YOU'VE
LEARNED FROM STARING DOWN THE NAKED OCCIPITAL LOBE
OR LOSING A PATIENT TO A RANDOM BASILAR ANEURYSM OR
HEARING THE NURSES AND RESIDENTS CHANGE SHIFTS FOR
THE NIGHT, THE VARIOUS RHYTHMS OF THE HOSPITAL, OR
THE SUICIDE OF YOUR HUSBAND, OR TRYING TO REACH YOUR
SONS BY RUINING YOUR BELONGINGS IN THE POOL?

Read these answers once again, but very slowly. Recite to
yourself, "I am alive."

architecture for monsters

roken Rib Cage rises above the desert of Abu Dhabi like a satanic cathedral.* The condominium tower is ninety-one stories of bleached-bone concrete curving from a sternum. This skeletal structure lacks the dancer's aplomb of a Calatrava: halfway up, steel beams wrench apart the façade, offering a glimpse into a courtyard that's so fecund, it's visceral. Critics have proclaimed it a magnum opus of feral genius, while others have mocked the aesthetic as "roadkill architecture." It is the most famous of the Damaged Organ buildings by Helen Dannenforth, an iconic, if controversial, doyenne of the field. Her sensibility has been lambasted as viciously

---

* "Broken Rib Cage" is the widely used nickname of the tower. The official but considerably lesser known title is Cleft Torso. Dannenforth has attempted to correct journalists and interviewers about this fact in the past only to be met with confusion; to spare herself the hassle, she, too, now refers to it as Broken Rib Cage.

carnal, if not outright bloodthirsty. "I was watching videos of surgeries," she said of her design. "As I saw doctors crack a man's chest and force a window to his heart, I was compelled to sketch."

It has been a good year for Dannenforth. A MacArthur fellowship was followed by a successful bid for the renovated Bilbao–Abando high-speed train station. The Met is putting on a retrospective of her work, a rarity for a living practitioner. Early access to the exhibition was like peering inside a cabinet of wonders. Here stood the presentation for her Memory of Skin pavilion at the Serpentine Gallery, a series of porous mesh panels rigged as the masts of a galleon upon which a plush, synthetic coral would grow via photocells. The artificial tissue would retain every indentation, every cicatrix incurred on its surface from human interaction before being removed at the end of the summer. There lay her drawings, done in brush pen with flourishes of watercolor, the details wrought with the precision of a miniaturist. Whispers circulate that she's the forerunner for the coveted Pritzker Prize. None of these accolades affect the woman herself, who in a few weeks will be fêted by friends and family in celebration of her fifty-fifth birthday.

I had the privilege to observe this feigned disaffection in person, when I interviewed Helen Dannenforth on Long Island, a few hours from the firm she founded in SoHo. Her Cumulus House ripples in contrast with the silhouettes of the surrounding manors. East Hampton commonly conjures visuals of rustic shingles salted by ocean winds, gambrel roofs, wraparound verandas, shuttered bay window seats. While she retained many of these elements—white trim, transomed doors—the classic cedar shakes have been changed to aluminum. As the pitched roof slopes into frothy formlessness, it's as cells replicating in a petri dish or the transition of rutted terrain to sky, those eponymous cumuli witnessed from the belly of a passenger jet. The house is a regression to precognition, to lying in her Michigan backyard as a child and staring up at sheets breezy on the line. It is an homage to laundry, weeds, naming clouds after the animals they resemble, power lines, suburbia, reverie.

"It's supposed to feel as if the house has become atmosphere," she explained. "I've been trying to tinker with softer constructions. Earlier in my career, my proposals were for buildings that had violence done to them. I was wary of the perception that I was merely feminine, too airy."

To become her employee has been likened more to taking holy orders than being hired for a job. The lucky are plucked from courses Dannenforth has taught at Harvard, Yale, and the Architectural Association in London. Acolytes are attired in monastic black or gray—de rigueur, but also required at Studio Forth by strict dress code. They muff their ears in huge headphones and don't speak unless necessary. Helen's wardrobe is part nun, part drag queen. A closet of monochromes surprises with the random attack of pigment. Gaudy statement jewelry scaffolds her knuckles and collarbone; she wears the opulence of her matriarch-white hair hanging like a large bellows between her shoulder blades. "They say people deface Rothko and Barnett Newman canvases because of their intense swaths of color," she told me, holding up a cocktail ensemble red as a spanking. "Wear something like this to both entice and threaten a man."

Not a single person in the community has heard her raise her voice, yet there is a pervasive fear of rousing her wrath. In general, she is unreadable, sibylline. "She shits ice cubes," said a former employee. It is rumored that she dismissed an assistant for expressing an opinion while in Zurich for a conference. The two were reclining in a sauna at Therme Vals, and the assistant quipped that Russian Suprematism was "paint-by-numbers for the blind." Helen shot back that she should pack her bags and return to the States. When, of course, this wasn't taken seriously and the assistant had the temerity to show her face at dinner, the table was made to wait to eat until she had been checked out of the hotel. Then again, to be a Dannenforth favorite is to gain a second mother, better than a mother. Those chosen few have spent holidays at her side. They have been counseled on their portfolios, their love lives, their childhoods. They have occupied rent-free the guest suite in her loft. Her protégées have also divulged that Helen, oblivious, has entered their rooms unannounced and had conversations about current projects as the protégée is nakedly lounging postcoitus with a paramour.

Romance isn't something that concerns Helen on a personal level, though she does have a daughter by an estranged ex-husband. Lily, sweet sixteen, came crashing in with keys, boots, and weekender bag during our chat over tea. It would have been easy to mistake her for the pubescent doppelgänger of her mother if not for the bits of leaves in her tangled hair, the *wabi-sabi* scratches and insect bites on her shins. She had gone on a camping trip with her boyfriend and unpacked by tossing makeup, snacks, tabloids, dirty clothes around the room like so much flotsam, the shipwreckage of a girl. "A girl becomes a woman when she learns everything has its place," Dannenforth aphorized. Only when she officially introduced us, when I wasn't distracted by this charming chaos, her sunburned cheeks reminiscent of hammocks and pitchers of lemonade and sneaked cigarettes, the effortless peasant blouse I'm certain cost hundreds of dollars, did I discern the asymmetry in her features that urged me to both look away and peer more closely, in thrall to its peculiarity.

The jaw was excruciatingly small and pulled to one side, as if she were frozen in an expression of trying to make up her mind about something or other. The mouth, despite its full lips with their pinup appeal, was similarly torqued. Helen, noticing how I stared but tried not to, swept the hair from her daughter's face and said, "You might as well see it all." An ear was pierced several times with studs; the opposite ear was proportionally sized but its ridges softened, as if it were sand on the beach washed over and flattened by the tides. Lily was born with craniofacial microsomia, classified as "severe" according to the grading scale known as OMENS. She had needed assistance even to breathe. When she was old enough, one of her ribs had been resected to supplement the absent bone of the jaw. Cartilage from that rib went to crafting her ear. The surgeons had been the best in the world. I could tell she would have been conventionally beautiful had she not suffered this anomaly in the womb, and she was still attractive, though mostly because she was compelling.

When the daughter went to use the shower, I dared to ask if Lily's condition has had any influence in Helen's notoriously ravaging style, her mangling of anatomy. The rib, the surgeries: How could it not have? "That's offensive," she replied. "I'm asked that because of my sex. If one of Frank Gehry's sons were disabled, would you ask if that had affected his concept development? My interest in the body began before I became a parent. It is primal. I don't have to use Lily for creative fodder. Remember what Juhani Pallasmaa wrote: 'The origin of our understanding of space lies in the cavern of the mouth.' I'm not the main practitioner with a corporeal bent, yet I am the one who is labeled a sociopath, a predator."

I never knew my mother. A lab tech assaulted and hid her in a cable chase of the Genetics Department at Berkeley. She was a molecular biologist studying drought resistance in strawberries. My father had a nervous breakdown after her death, so at twenty months old I was sent to live with my maternal grandparents. I cultivated my mother's passion for structure, but turned to architecture in lieu of science. Dannenforth was my heroine, a female authority in a profession hostile to estrogenic influence. Certain coincidences in our biographies—our motherlessness, abandonment by a father—also helped the flourishing of my worship, I admit. When Helen came to give a lecture at Rice, where I was pursuing a master's, I waited to speak with her in the hall outside the auditorium. Once she addressed me, I muttered some phrase of thanks and fled, too filled with anxiety to permit her to become real.

Soon afterward, I dropped out of my graduate program. My grandmother was diagnosed with Alzheimer's, and I returned to sell the house and set her up in an assisted-living facility. I was the sum total of extant kin—my dad, remarried, hadn't reclaimed custody. Boxes of knickknacks and mementos were the raw materials from which I constructed the model of my mother. Gardens were her solace, as were birds. Pads of paper were filled with graphite nests, their twiggy tessellation like the still life of a tornado. It occurred to me that a nest is the epitome of dwellings, a safe haven between firmament and roots. There was a metaphysical warmth to the belongings I sorted through, as if I sensed spirits lingering under afghans, doing dishes, slamming the screen door the way she had as a child and later the way I did as a child.

At any rate, I freelanced laser-cut shelving and patio extensions. I also wrote articles. Finally, that fortuitous day arrived when I was commissioned for a profile piece by the seminal

Inhabit. Helen failed to recognize me, which wasn't demoralizing. Too cowardly to mention we had already met, I segued into her research on family estates, hoping she would reveal her past.

"I lift from gothic novels," she said. "There's something about the entropic vision of an ancient manor that's both creepy and welcoming. We treat architecture how we treat our physical selves, as doomed to oblivion. No effort is spared in restoring the Sistine Chapel ceiling to its pristine éclat. A Matisse won't go to waste. Take a Mies van der Rohe, though, and it's given the care of a crypt. Preservation's a Sisyphean task in this craft."

She waxed melancholy about the replicas of Japanese and German villages fabricated from scratch in the 1940s to test the incendiary capacity of napalm. Hollywood set directors outfitted each domicile down to the details of toiletries and authentic newspapers. "Extraordinary amounts of effort for the simulacra of ghost towns that were then blown up," Helen lamented. "Sounds about right." Discussing books rekindled the embers of her monologue. In her office, Ernst Neufert's handbook on ergonomic principles rests alongside *The Castle of Otranto*, *The Woman in White*, and *Jane Eyre* with its crazy wife in the attic. Recondite chambers and whimsical, old-timey chicanery are her fetishes. "Any shelter should also expose us. I'm a fan of that genre of literature because passages of prose describe passages through ramparts, hedge mazes, and servants' quarters. The plot hinges on a secret in a secret room. It makes visible how the brain harbors a secret."

Helen has her own cache of secrets. In upstate New York, on acres of rolling hills, woods, and manicured demesne, at an institution titled "the Retreat," lives a patient named Hannah Dannenforth: her half sister. My interview had bombed. I was in the doldrums. At the end of a drive in a rental car without a working radio, largely spent feeling sorry for myself, I sat down in the Rec Center across from a woman who looked like everybody's aunt. Where Helen was lissome, Hannah was plump; where Helen's hair was loosely elegant, Hannah's was tightly cropped and turfing every which way, like a lawn in severe need of mowing; where Helen entertained in haute couture, Hannah hid in stained secondhand. "Do you know why I'm stuck here with a bunch of junkies and schizophrenics and Adirondack chairs?" she asked. I said that I didn't—sleuthing out her contact information itself had been a test of will. "I'm here," she replied, "because I'm Lily's real mother."

Of course, that isn't the reason she was committed. She kidnapped Lily, twelve years old at the time. Hannah agreed to a plea deal: years of probation on a suspended sentence, provided that she voluntarily check into a psychiatric hospital. "There's buildings dedicated to locking up people like me for good," she said. "I bet you don't hear my sister talk about the architecture of the prison, of the sanatorium, do you?" She went on, "Helen blames me for Lily. When she looks at her, she sees her biggest failure. I was afraid while I was pregnant that I would birth one of those babies with microcephaly or intestines spilling out of their bodies. But after I saw her, those feelings seemed trivial. When I look at that girl, I feel proud. I think: I made her. She's mine."

According to Hannah, Lily was in on the abduction. Surreptitious emails and phone calls were exchanged. A lot of kids want to run away, I argued, but that doesn't mean you take them up on the offer. "This wasn't about hating your mother because she grounded you during spring vacation," she retorted. This was about the sanctity of the shared meal, report cards pinned on the refrigerator and pinwheels in flower pots, coercing the dog into a costume for funny snaps, a home for which the sole purpose wasn't to be a spread in a magazine. Yes, disappearing had been drastic, but Helen had been indifferent when Hannah was laid off, when medical bills piled up, when her property was foreclosed. She was living out of her car, "the Traveling Spinster." She was forbidden to see Lily. Plus, legal recourse wasn't available to her, because she had signed away her rights. I found myself confiding in her as I had wanted to confide in her sister. "I know how it feels," she said, her voice wistful, intimate, "to have lost all that you cherish."

Hannah was incantatory as an oracle as she described their route past pine tree nurseries, fields knuckled with gourds, billboards blistered on blue vistas, factories weathered as yesterday's newspaper. Here was the alleged heartland.* Novelty, for me, has always been accompanied by the orchestra of longing. When I saw the Duomo in Florence, when I went on an elementary class trip to gaze upon the pharaohs in their sarcophagi, wonder harmonized with the wonder of why an anonymous man murdered my mother. I wished I could share these marvels with her, or at least tell her about them, and her abiding kindness would make them possible, explicable, but she was gone, which also seemed impossible, and the sensation of encountering the miraculous was diminished with anguish. So I didn't dare skeptically pause this story of a reunion so like the sort I had fantasized about and would forever be denied.

"I forgot the appetite the world has for girls," Hannah told me. At a McDonald's in Ohio, they hunkered down to enjoy the heat-lamped potpourri of starch and ketchup packets and antiseptic, the crumpling of oiled wrappers, when a yellow bus unloaded a bunch of troublemakers into the parking lot.

---

* America is an idea that there is more space where nobody is than where anybody is, so said Gertrude Stein, herself a nurturer of great talent under her tent of personality. "There are vast tracts in this nation that are beyond vacant space, they're degraded space, zombie space. It's the pastoral of the forlorn mini mall," Helen pontificated. We were on the topic of the factory she built in North Carolina for HUSK, the high-end furniture manufacturer. It is caterpillarean, raised up on disembodied legs, looking to crawl away over the terrain in an instant. When the company went out of business, it was converted into a museum of artifacts endemic to the United States: slot machines based on horror films, the face of our Savior inscribed on toast and sundry pastries, toilet seat mosaics. "A region that has been populated and then forgotten triggers sentimentality, which is why we have a predilection for kitsch. It's funny how everything has to prove that it is what it is."

Immediately Lily was surrounded by backpacks. They played with her hair, caressed her ear, asked her to smile, and giggled at her lopsided grin. Someone produced a temporary tattoo of a butterfly. There were cries of, "Put it on her face!" She contorted head over shoulder in the bathroom to scrutinize the result, planted just below her jaw. "It's ugly," she decided. Soaping thoroughly, she scrubbed until it was bits of torn wings and her neck was red. That children would be casually cruel was one matter, the attention of grown men another. They stopped at a desert gas station. A wind sock flopped overhead, desolate as the horizon. When Lily went in search of Twizzlers and Slim Jims, truckers were mesmerized by her ass. "Girl," they hollered, as if they were this moment catching on to the names for things.*

As their flight continued, Hannah worried more about her daughter's safety and less about being apprehended. Winded from the switchbacks of the Rockies, they rented a room that led out to a pool in a hotel with clinical depression. The soullessness of these suites—the oily genital smears on the mirrors, the matching TVs, duvets—was an uncanny source

---

* A woman can't mess up, Helen said. It's like when you're a girl and you're told you summoned your own disaster. "I have to work alone. Women are cheated in the partnerships of our industry. Eileen Gray and the E-1027 villa is the foremost instance. Le Corbusier saw it and was smitten, so without asking for permission, he painted murals on the immaculate walls. She was furious. It was a violation. This architectural pissing act caused the press to credit it to him. I suppose there's justice in the fact that he had this restless fascination with the machinery of aviation but did not die in the air. While he was swimming his daily laps, he drowned right by that villa."

of comfort.* In the morning, Lily was missing, her twin bed a maelstrom of blankets. She wasn't devouring gummy pancakes at the buffet. She wasn't off taking the car for a joyride. Back in their uncaring accommodations, her sad, middle-aged would-be-felon mom assumed the traditional pose of defeat, cradling her head. Then the baritone hum of the air conditioner switched off, and she heard glass-dulled laughter that she must have tuned out before.

Lily was at the center of a group of teens goofing around by the "out of order" diving platform. Their ease had the quality of established friendships, though Hannah knew they were but the tenuous bonds of chlorine and Coppertone. A boy dipped below the surface and burst forth with Lily on his shoulders. Not pausing to deliberate, an opposing couple did the same. Both boys strutted, enjoying the ruffled crotches against their necks, the spandex cleavage grazing their buzz cuts. They waded nearer and nearer until the girls began to grapple the air like trees come to life in a nightmarish forest, if trees could also be girls. Lily fought viciously and below the belt—yanking braids, ramming shoulders, lunging for bikini tops. She bested team after team until the last girl fell, the thunk of an elbow to the skull and the subsequent splash the signaling bell of defeat.

"She won because she's a freak," the loser declared, climbing

---

* Helen Dannenforth, too, has a fondness for the contradiction inherent to hubs of transit, which is why that train station in Spain will branch like dissected capillaries and arteries to dramatize the many pathways of a voyage.

up the ladder. A scratch crosshatched a string of her suit and blurred with moisture. "Look, I'm bleeding." Runoff swished onto the deck to the rhythm of her hips like a fluid hula skirt. The rest of the girls joined her, hiving into a clique on reclining chairs and scrunching their hair dry. "Is that it?" Lily challenged them. The boys, unwilling to upset the girls, drifted toward the shallow end.

"Lily saw our relationship differently after that," Hannah said. Waving grandly for her daughter's attention and to subvert her ostracism, she yelled, "Lily! Lily!" This move, however, was met with epiphanic mortification on Lily's part, as if she had been the one to hit the water with a slap. The future had shifted. A glamorous mother like Helen at Lily's side recontextualized the difference of her features as sexy or mysterious. A mother like Hannah, with a paisley nightgown tucked into her jeans and pressure socks, would make Lily a regular mistake of biology.

Now Lily had questions. What was my mother like growing up?

"She was mean. Helen's ten years older," Hannah said, "so when she was roped into babysitting, she raided the liquor cabinets and poured alcohol down my throat. Sometimes she kicked, pinched, or hit me."

But was she pretty? Was she popular?

"She was out of control. After she and some friends burned down a derelict cabin, she got off easy, in my opinion, when she was enrolled in a boarding school. I think they were

78

really afraid that she would get pregnant out of wedlock like her real mother."

Why does she hate you?

"Back then, if a girl accidentally got knocked up, her only option was to have the baby in secret while ostensibly visiting relatives in the Upper Peninsula. That's how Helen was born. Our father didn't even know she existed. He found out when she was around eight, and initiated contact. He didn't intend to fall in love with my mother, Helen's stepsister; it sort of happened. Can't you imagine Helen lying awake in her dormitory and resenting me?"

Am I like her?

"I told Lily that she shouldn't want to be. Helen was battling a lot of demons—I know that now, though I didn't then. She was packed up and moved between our house and her adopted parents' house like baggage. I suppose that the ordeal did turn her into a genius."

This apologia was gratifying to Lily, who confessed she had been skipping class, smoking pot, allowing herself to be fondled by boys. "I was nauseous with jealousy, that Lily was fascinated by my narcissistic half sister but not me"—that she aspired to toss her innocence away in imitation. Helen was the chosen mother because she was distant, unknowable. Though isn't everyone, in a sense?*

---

* In a study of unknowability, Studio Forth was commissioned for a church in France at the base of the Jura Mountains. It is a dome of obscure dimensions, a cocoon of mist sourced from Lake Bourget. Inside, a plexiglass column extends

Utah brought a bed-and-breakfast run by Mormons, a ma-
tron with a forehead smooth from piety carrying towels upstairs. "I'm not sure about you," she said, "but I don't feel like
I've arrived somewhere until I've had a wash." In the morning, a kitchen with a bona fide family greeted them, cool
scrambled eggs in a warm majolica bowl, bacon scalloped like
a petticoat on a porcelain plate, toast with honey, toast with
butter, toast with marmalade. The father drank coffee in a fa-
therly way. It was a rare lay indulgence. A couple girls around
Lily's age laid out place settings, methodically circling like the
hands of a clock. As for Lily, she had draped a gossamer wrap
around her head, in defiance of the heat. It wasn't like her to
take pains to hide her face. Reading comics, calm in the middle of the endearing storm of preparations, was why: a boy,
tall, blond, fresh as a seraph in a fresco, his awareness limited
to the nimbus of his own importance.

"When are you due on the road?" the father asked. The
salt-of-the-earth wife chimed in to suggest a detour to the salt
flats, if they weren't in a hurry. They could spare an afternoon
to be tour guides, pack a lunch, et cetera. With the family
involved—i.e., the son—it was obvious that Lily was keen on
the scheme, so Hannah consented, repeating a mantra that

---

to an oculus through which water is poured and frozen, then the plexiglass removed. The notion was Cartesian. If the soul was like a wax, recognizable as a
paraffin taper or a melted padella, god could be understood as hydrogen—as vapor,
as solid, and as liquid after a chilling encounter. The column has to be continually
replaced, since it is suspended in an endless process of wearing away from a patina
of fingerprints.

such acts of concession, like daily prayers, would win over her daughter.

A minivan spun them to where the landscape blanched. Wasn't the Dead Sea also a saline promised land? It was inevitable, then, that a tribe of faithful would settle there, by God's blankness. The trunk was unloaded, gingham spread against the white, along with tinfoiled wedges of tuna and wheat, grapes, seltzer, plastic utensils. There was a scooping of chips into an avocado, then it was a ripe reminder on the paper plate.

Benjamin, the boy, bounced a tennis ball off a racket while his greyhound watched in anticipation, curved like the handle of a water pump. He got around to throwing the ball for the dog, which left divots as it ran with a puff puff puff of crust. Lily paid attention to Benjamin by way of the dog.

"What a wholesome family you are," Hannah mused. "We try to raise our kids with proper values, to say 'please' and 'thank you,' to listen to their elders, to treat the body as a temple," the father replied. "I thought people preached that the body is a temple to prevent girls from living in theirs," Hannah countered. "Female or not," he said, "if they don't respect themselves, then who will?" The sisters screamed, "Benji! Lunch! Lunch! Benji!" until he jogged in their direction. Dutifully, Lily accompanied him, a shadow of his shadow, but as she closed in, the wind kited her careful wrap into the air. She didn't move, as though if she didn't, no one would notice.

There was a struggle against tears, then the tears. The wrap had landed on the crepitant grate of the van, so Benjamin went to the rescue, mumbling to her, "Here you go," as he offered it up, crudely folded. "That fabric is so pretty," the older girl said. "Where did you buy it?" the younger asked. They sat her down, untangled the fringe, and rearranged the wrap around her neck. The boy scarfed his food and was off, but Lily let him go solo. He adventured a long distance, the pale dog in alto-relievo over the pale dust. On the ride back, the sisters quarreled and the mother warned that she would confiscate their cell phones; meanwhile, Benjamin irritated almost everyone by thrusting his knees into the seats. During departure, the girls hugged tentatively as girls do, avoiding a pressing of breasts yet with genuine affection. Lily blatantly ignored the boy as he said goodbye.

The family was like a saintly family with their haloes turned up too bright as they waved in the headlights. Passing through Vegas, Lily relinquished the silence she had been fattening to say, "This is the brightest city astronauts can locate in orbit." There was the replica of the Eiffel Tower, the pyramid of the Luxor with its fake Sphinx, the Doric-columned Caesar's Palace. Miles out, where lodging was cheap, they checked into Motel Apocalypse, a science-fiction vision of the future from the past, each room a unique calamity.

The apocalypse they picked was a virus-ravaged colony on the moon, a lunar Roanoke, though the Rapture was debated.

"This is stupid," Lily complained, throwing herself on the bed in the way of girls who yet throw their limbs too hard at objects, before they're indoctrinated in modesty, into taking up as little space as they can. As Hannah knelt to offer comfort, brushing cheek against cheek, she felt shaky, sacrilegious. It was the first time they had touched since setting out, and while she knew they had time, nothing but time, it also felt like she would never be good enough for her daughter. She'd had the same feeling when holding her in the hospital for the first time. "No one will ever love me," Lily moaned into her pillow. Kissing her on the slope of her nape, Hannah said, "Not true." If Lily wasn't good enough for Helen, and Hannah wasn't good enough for Lily, but Helen wasn't good enough for Hannah's family, was there anyone who was suited for each other? Later that night, police escorted her from Motel Apocalypse; strobes revolved in the lobby like a junior high dance.

That Lily was missing turned out to be a revelation to Helen. She was overseas in Beijing, supervising the foundation pour for her labyrinthine concert hall, cochlear like an ear ("too literal," said its detractors) with a tympanic, abalone outer shell. What must Lily have made of such a design? If she saw it as her mother mocking her, she had reason to rebel. Those mandated with her care had been strategically confused as to the girl's whereabouts: the housekeeper believed her to be staying with a friend, her driver that she was off with

family, which was, of course, accurate. When Lily phoned
from Nevada, complaining that Hannah had kidnapped her
and how much it sucked, Helen alerted law enforcement and
didn't bother to buy a plane ticket. She was needed at the site.
"Lily betrayed me," Hannah said, but if life is occasionally interesting in anecdote, it's not in the actual living, and she was
worn down by forgiveness. After all, Lily was a child, and children are still subject to the whims of their boredoms. "Why
do we have children? I kept asking myself that question. We
can't protect them—not with our infrastructures, our technology, our culture. They're going to die. They're also going
to intentionally and unintentionally hurt each other. It's selfish to have children."

Strangulation as indicated by a fractured hyoid was the
cause of my mother's death. She had been raped. The coroner folded open her skin like a map, emptied the cadaver—or
rather, the body of evidence that was my mother—of parts,
and stitched her shut with a sailmaker's needle, while painstakingly recording the bruises, the cuts and abrasions, the
vaginal swelling into a microphone. I related to what Hannah
was saying about procreation, though what were those of
us who were already alive to do? "Love," she said. "Love as
much as you can. Lily may not feel my love yet, but she will.
I even love Helen." She seemed to have been oversaturated
with therapy. Platitudes were for pharmacies and embroidery.
Still, the truth is that love doesn't vanish. When you love, she
postulated, it stays with the beloved for life, passes into those

they love, and unspools through the universe, expanding with it into eternity.

I wanted to believe that my mother had loved me and would have continued to do so, but I didn't feel her love. If I searched for it enough, perhaps I would find that emotional inheritance, hidden somewhere inside myself like an appendix, an organ I didn't know was there, or why I needed it, until it ruptured. Is that the reason, during my drive back to the city in the saddest rental car on earth, why I fantasized about every tiny detail of that miserable Hannah-Lily odyssey? I wasn't sure what I was writing anymore, as certainly my editors at the glossy coffee-table magazine wouldn't publish this mess of an article and risk pissing off a starchitect like Dannenforth, one of the most powerful among the elite set awarded that portmanteau. The interview would have to serve as another bit of paper I crumpled up or tore apart and added to the model of my mother—perhaps, after this piece, that nest would finally be complete, and, just as I had been able to do with her before she was killed, I could curl up inside of it and be nurtured.

The fifty-fifth birthday party for Helen Dannenforth was held at Cumulus House. Helen was right—in the fey evening light, augmented with globule lamps in various colors and shaped like overgrown alien plants, these environs did indicate the evolution of a tender ideology. A recent installation of hers at the Tate Modern was similar in tone. Suspended alveolar sacs gave visitors the chance to climb inside the knitted webbing and sway, read, or nap for whatever duration they wished. A faint respiratory rhythm was also broadcast throughout Turbine Hall to impart the sensation of nestling within a pair of lungs. "I was charmed that tourists and commuters, away from their cubicles on lunch, would let down their guard in a public space the same as a private one," she had said. The ambience was somehow oddly sterile. In search of her among her guests, I navigated a bespoke obstacle course of bankers, effete photographers with their gallerina companions, architects in thick glasses like a second pair of eyebrows layered over their eyebrows, and lazy cognoscenti.

They talked about art that has inspired architecture, architecture that has inspired film, literature that has inspired architecture, architecture that has inspired literature, musicians who have inspired artists who have inspired architects, arcane illustrations of vivisectionists and botanists that have inspired architecture, how psychoanalysis has influenced architecture and how architecture influences psychology, architecture during war and architecture during peace, the architecture of fashion, the architecture of cuisine, the architecture of children's toys. They talked about the obsolescence of libraries, movie theaters, and journalism. They talked about curators and what would happen to a curatorial vocation in the digital era. They talked about innovation—thermal metals that breathe like a rubbery shark pelt, printing customizable chairs with fungi, neon electric tattoos that would blush with a touch. They talked about the weather. They talked about the parties they had been to and how boring those parties were and the parties they planned on attending and how boring those parties would be.

I observed Helen as she clung to her latest darling. As they mingled together with each group of guests, he ensured she was well lubricated with wine, smiled benignly but not enough to be ingratiating, mentioned a story he had heard on public radio. She was gracious, but also intimidating as per normal in a backless Chanel dress, Hermès bangles, and Louboutin heels. Despite her favorite's ministrations, he was inadequate to stop her increasing unsteadiness on those heels. They dug into a patch of sod and she stepped out of them. Their two red soles stranded in the grass looked like the undersides of tongues. Conversations drifted on to the topic of the hostess, on whether she was sleeping with that attractive man she was mentoring ("They're very cozy"), whether she had slept with past mentees ("They tend to be male"), whether she was sleeping with her ex-husband ("No, he's investigating the tribal beats of Balinese rain drum music in Indonesia"), whether she had slept with a Saudi prince when she was in the Middle East ("He gave her Lorraine Schwartz earrings worth a mil").

Ensconced in a corner by the alfresco bar were Lily and her boyfriend, a reedy, nondescript kid in a Horace Mann blazer. She didn't budge from her position or speak unless addressed point-blank, though he frequently sallied forth, a bougie hunter-gatherer, in order to bring back heaping portions of artisanal junk food—burgers, chicken strips, fish sandwiches—with a variety of "deconstructed" aiolis. "She's drunk," Lily said, implicating her mother with a glance, and ushered him into the house. At an unsuspicious distance, I tailed them—I had something to give her, for her and no one else. They evaded me behind a closed door upstairs, so instead of interrupting, I snooped. Alas, it was as expected—the medications, the thread count—though in an underwear drawer I did find a gleaming chrome dildo that resembled less a dildo than a Brâncuși or a parametric mockup of a bridge or spaceship. Although perhaps I perceived it so because of the person to whom it belonged. Briefly, I contemplated stealing the dildo. For the rest of my life, I'd display it and pronounce, "This dildo used to pleasure Helen Dannenforth."

A voice accused, "I understand you met with Hannah." Her feet were muddy and her chignon was straggly, so the yin-yang roles were reversed, and Helen, one of the few women renowned for her talents these days, was now the fully grown doppelgänger of her daughter returning from a camping trip.

"I did," I replied.

Unfortunately, that meant that she or a member of her staff would have to sign off on what I had written before it went to print.

Such a demand was unethical and a bit insulting, I communicated without thinking, simultaneously taken aback by my attitude. I could have told her I no longer planned to publish.

Perhaps, I recommended, she or a member of her staff preferred to pen the entire article? I was slightly light-headed during this confrontation, like it was a high. At least now I would be seen by her, albeit negatively. The sentiments expressed by her sister, I said, might strike her as a very welcome repentance.

"I'm guessing she told you she has ultimately overcome the wounding at the core of her identity or guileless id or what have you in order to walk a healing path of forgiveness," she replied, buoyed by rage. "She also said that the meaning of life is love, am I correct? This isn't some unsung epiphany. She's a pathological liar." Who paid for her indefinite stay at "the Retreat," essentially a spa where she can whine about how wronged she feels? Helen paid, though she didn't have to, and Hannah was deemed just fine, perfectly sane, although, she added, extremely manipulative. Who spent that "road trip" with Lily insinuating that Helen had been abusive toward Hannah when they were growing up and so on? The worst, however, was the reminiscing about her pregnancy and manipulating newcomers like me into believing that Hannah is Lily's "real" mother and that Helen maliciously hindered them from having a relationship.

"My Lily is my Lily." Lily was her genetic daughter. Hannah had been the surrogate, after recourses of IVF, acupuncture, herbal steam baths, pro-uterine diets, and pretty much every snake-oil remedy under the sun had failed. She supported her half sister on account of vestigial gratitude. "How you cope with loneliness determines whether you are strong or weak, particularly if you are a woman," she said. "Hannah isn't equipped to cope." Sad as that was, Helen wasn't about to let Hannah turn her daughter against her. I stood inarticulate, at a loss. When I interviewed Helen, it felt fake, rehearsed. There was no vulnerability, no spontaneous insight. Hannah was scrupulously candid, as exposed as a decomposing shack in the wilderness. "My responses were premeditated," was her justification, "in that I'm constantly meditating upon what responses I would give to questions. Don't blame the subject for your poor skill."

She could tell I was intelligent, but my values were droll, conventional. "There isn't one blueprint for how to build a life. Character and family are also constructions." This advice of hers wasn't new, either. Architecture can insidiously rank and organize us: from medieval thatched cottages where everyone slept communally on a straw dais and if there were extramarital shenanigans, well, it had to have been that roguish incubus, to our contemporary thrall to individualism borne out in individualistic enclosures like the capsule pods in Tokyo or microapartments in Manhattan. Each individual requires their own tiny niche, their own luminous screen to satellites, social media. "We have separated ourselves out," Helen has said in previous interviews, "as the home was separated out in the Industrial Revolution. What was the source of work, play, sex, the gamut, has been butchered and sold off piecemeal as chops and steaks."

Neither I nor society at large—strangers—had the privilege to judge how she raised her daughter—such judgment was evil—or how she demonstrated her love. "Thoroughly fact-check your story before it appears in *Inhabit*. Oh, and if you were scouring my house for a souvenir, feel free to have whatever you like from my stuff."

After my first tête-à-tête with Helen, I had a disturbing dream—please pardon me for sharing. A woman went through an excruciating metamorphosis. Her sinews stretched, her bones elongated into a suprascaffolding, her joints a joinery. She towered in agony. I roamed her muscular corridors, investigating the warp and thrum of a high-rise circulating with lymph, hemoglobin, nerves, hormones. It was a monstrous architecture, an architecture for monsters, an attempt by her to accommodate tenants who would never believe she had done enough. We take for granted that our mothers accept whatever risks to bear us, that they would die for us, or that they otherwise gladly sacrifice for us their quotidian hours, days, and weeks, but this is a fallacy. If children are born or become cruel and reproducing is a vice, as Hannah Dannenforth suggested, perhaps it is not because it is in our nature, but because we too easily forget the distinct identities of our mothers.

Hannah had composed a letter that I said I would pass along to Lily. I tore the envelope and convinced myself that I was reading to ascertain that she wasn't trying to abscond with her again, but I was reading it as a cipher for myself. Would my brilliant, dead mother have loved or resented me? Would I have loved her?

I slipped it under Lily's door after reading these words:

"Did you know, my dearest daughter, that in sanatoriums and prisons there are classes in designing your ideal house? We request catalogs, tiles, and swatches from area stores. I've been at leisure to ruminate on it, and the house I would build for you would be a phenomenon of staircases and country stars, great fires burning in a stone hearth. It will be sprawling, but not so sprawling that if you shout, there's a danger of not receiving an answer. Nooks and crannies are scattered around for when dinner is served but you're not ready yet. An attic holds trunks with crystal globes of your memories. You'll be able to list all the plants that spike like cuneiform in the garden. Perhaps it's along the coast of the sea—or no, in the mountains—or its own island, or poised above a city like Siena or Buenos Aires or Istanbul. You can't reach the house unless it's by boat or dirigible. The forecast reflects your mood—rainy when you want it to rain, sunny when you want sun, in the midst of a blizzard when you want to feel your sanctuary is a sanctuary. Within brisk walk or bicycle, there will be a quaint grocery store and anything you seek—a salon, an arcade, a haunted orchard—and a Benjamin who adores you. There's more, but what I hope you see is that we would be happy."

the promised hostel

Carl is a bipolar orthopedic podiatrist, and he's fussy at the nipple. He's been on a nursing strike for the past several days, and Maddy is worried that she's doing something wrong. She massages a breast, priming the milk for him. After a few false starts, he's able to latch. "Gently, Carl," she coos. "This isn't a race." Seung Hun rolls in wearing fuzzy slippers and some kind of kimono. He is multitalented. He's got a trust fund back in Sydney in addition to being an asshole. He goes to town on Maddy's unoccupied breast and finishes in under a minute, not too tough to satisfy. There are eight of us. Every morning, the buffet table is abundant with cheese, butter, olives, eggs, tomatoes, cucumbers, bread, jam, honey, yogurt, and fresh coffee and tea, but the men prefer Maddy. It is a hostel in the biblical promised land, the promised hostel, but not for me. I am in love with her. And I am the only one not allowed to drink from her breasts.

I follow Maddy to her room after breakfast. We all have our own rooms after complaining long enough about Carl waking us up by jumping on the bed during his manic episodes. It's the off-season, and the staff wants to ensure our happiness. Maddy swears she hasn't been fucking any of the expat backpackers, but I don't believe her.

"You know," she shouts, "I can see you hiding out there in the bushes. Why don't you come in and tell me what you want?"

"Maddy," I say, standing in her doorway. "Madeline." Maybe the extra syllables will help my case. "Can I have a taste?"

"I'm sorry, sugar," she says, "but I'm all drained dry."

At noon, Reginald and the Professor stand guard over the samovar, waiting for it to boil, while Maddy offers Liam his usual midday snack. It was Liam who started this whole mess. A few days after Maddy's arrival, he began bawling as he related to her that he was traveling the world on the last of his dead mother's savings. She laid his head against her nightgown and told him to hush. He dropped crocodile tears into her lacy décolletage, and she urged him to nurse. Pretty soon, all the backpackers had sob stories or problems of some sort for which Maddy's milk was the sweet elixir of relief. That was weeks ago.

Liam is a teenager from Quebec and he has disgusting

ginger dreads and he doesn't yet know what it means to be alive. Like clockwork, when Maddy's milk runs out now, he buries his face between her cleavage and cries. He also gets the hiccups. He cries and hiccups at the same time. Reginald watches them with longing. Reginald is a speech pathologist from London who struggles with his own stutter, and he might even be more in love with Madeline than I am. The Professor, whose real name I have forgotten, has no family or friends or connection to any living person from what we can determine, as if he simply manifested here spontaneously as the archetype of lonely gentleman scholar. He's an elderly fellow from South Africa with a cane and a limp and a wizard beard and he's got a fancy Oxbridge doctorate and he teaches English literature at some university in Ankara. Madeline burps Liam and rubs his back. "There, there, sweet pea," she says. She begins to sing a lullaby. The melody soothes him. "That's better," Maddy whispers. "Why don't you go play with the other boys?"

Liam skips out the door in search of Seung Hun, whom he adores, though Seung Hun can only be bothered to toss him the occasional sardonic scrap. I close my leather journal and am hot in pursuit. I know they're probably off to smoke more of Liam's dead mom's stash of medicinal marijuana in the ruins. As I walk toward the amphitheater, I tear at the words I've written and scatter them along the path. I've been shedding language since my arrival in Çirali—a sentence here, the inchoate jangle of a phrase there, though sometimes only the indiscriminate coughing up of solitary nouns and verbs is all I can manage.

"The big bunk room smells like lactic farts and low self-esteem."

I hid that sentence beneath Carl's pillow some months ago. He never found it, for all I know.

"The most intimate aspect of skin is its temperature," I stashed in the empty bowels of a Roman sarcophagus.

As I wade through the riverbed toward the rubble, "je-june," "belletristic," and "estuary" fly into the wind from my fingertips. They bleed in the water.

Seung Hun lies stretched out on a grassy knoll at the center of the amphitheater, still in his fuzzy slippers and kimono, but with the front flaps flung open and his genitals exposed to open air.

"How's the novel coming, mate?" he asks. "Here, have some weed."

"It's fine," I say and pluck the blunt from his fingers. "Slow."

"What's it about, anyway?" Liam chimes in, lounging between one of the rows of stone seats. For some reason, he has also taken off his pants. Word has gotten out, it seems, that I am writing the next great American novel set on the Turkish coast.

"It's about a man looking back on the choice he made as a youth, which he now realizes has defined the rest of his life, between an older woman with a lot of sexual experience and a young girl who was just as naïve as he was."

"What female does he pick?" Liam asks.

"Neither."

"Sounds stupid," Seung Hun replies, rolling over in the grass so his bare buttocks face the sun.

"Hey, I heard that Jørgen had sex with Maddy," I offer.

"When?" Liam asks.

"Says who?" Seung Hun asks.

They both sit up.

If Maddy is fucking one of the backpackers, the most likely candidate would be Jørgen, a Norwegian Tantric sex instructor. At dawn, we've seen him walking through the ruins to the beach with yoga mat in tow, his stride so long we could leapfrog from footprint to footprint. He will meditate and stretch there for hours and return to instruct us with phrases like, "*Ja*, you must run toward your fear, my friends," and "Your pain is your finest teacher," or he will fondly reminisce about all the women he's trained in the art of spiritual lovemaking. His mother raised him to the age of twelve in an ashram, where everyone communally swapped fluids in a room of dirty mattresses and then went outside to experiment with punching each other in the face. Now he's the head of the Northern European committee on eco-villages, as well as a fuck god. He is blond-haired and blue-eyed, with muscles so defined I feel like I should take gravestone rubbings of them, and he has a pecker the size of a fjord, and I hate his oversized Scandinavian guts.

"That's just the rumor," I reply.

"You're full of it," Liam says, after a while. "Maddy wouldn't do that to us."

"She's still not letting you near her tits, is she?" Seung Hun asks. If they knew the ways I had been intimate with Maddy in years past, they might be less inclined to pity me. We haven't bothered to tell them—something about her nouveau earth-mother mystique has turned it into a secret.

"What is it like?" I ask.

"It's sweet," Liam says.

"Richer than cow's milk," Seung Hun says.

"It depends on the day, too," Liam says.

"That's true," Seung Hun says. "Like, if Maddy ate a lot of that *döner kebab* the night before, the milk will be more savory."

"Meaty," Liam says.

"That doesn't sound appetizing," I say.

"Her tits are perfect," Liam says.

"Better than Soo Yeon's bosom?" I ask Seung Hun.

"No woman's tits will ever match Soo Yeon's bosom," he says, "or her coy smile, her hair so dark it's almost indigo. When I see how she moves about a room, I want to take her in my arms. I go crazy watching her paint those adorable baby toes while tanning by the pool. Sometimes she takes off her top and asks me to apply lotion on her back. Lotion!"

Seung Hun stands up and he's got a chubby. It tells the time of day in the amphitheater like a sundial. Bits of grass and dirt are stuck in the sweaty turf of his chest, his pubic hair, the fuzzy pink slippers.

"Soo Yeon!" he bellows to the cheap seats, spreading his arms wide. "You are a goddess! Hear me, one and all! I confess! I want to kill my father and marry my mother!"

Soo Yeon isn't really Seung Hun's mother, obviously. She's a famous actress who walked into his father's plastic surgery practice. Seung Hun's father is perhaps the most sought-after cosmetic doctor in Seoul. After he opened Soo Yeon's skin with a scalpel, he married her. Seung Hun's real mother, fed up with being bombarded by the billboards of her husband's new wife, moved to Australia with her little boy to live among relatives. Ever since, Seung Hun has flown back and forth between the two countries, slavishly doting on Soo Yeon with gifts and trinkets, emails and letters, perfumed odes that he hides among her things. That is, until he got banned from his father's mansion for a reason that he won't reveal.

It's Jørgen's turn for a ration from Maddy during dinner. We listen to him lapping as we pick at plates of eggplant and lamb. It makes us uncomfortable. He refuses to nurse like everybody else and feels compelled to plant delicate kisses around her areolae. I can tell by the way he breastfeeds that he thinks he's so special. What exactly is he trying to prove? Does he imagine he's doing this for Maddy's benefit? For ours? Seung Hun sits like a sultan on a throne of tasseled pillows, sending text after text into the ether, until he steps outside in his robe and slippers to place a call. In the same corner Carl is on his laptop trying to video-chat his daughter without the knowledge of his wife.

"Emily, honey," he says, "do you remember what I taught you—to erase the history once we're done talking?"

"Yes, Dad," crackles through the speakers. Carl plugs in headphones and Emily's words are lost to me.

"Good girl," he says. "Now, if you hear Mom coming down the stairs, I don't even want you to say goodbye. I want you to end the chat and erase the history. Do you understand? You never spoke to Dad."

The Professor is playing backgammon with Liam on the ottoman. He recites lines by nineteenth century French poets while waiting for the kid to lose. I try to focus on their conversation instead of the moist smacks and swallows of Jørgen at the boob or Reginald masticating his lamb. Reginald always chooses a spot close to me, probably because the presence of the journal gives him the impression he doesn't need to break his silence. Since he cannot help but mangle his morphemes, the use of language is occasioned by only the utmost necessity. For this reason, he seems to delight in mealtimes, his tongue and teeth and gullet at least a utility for digestion. I try to picture his lips on a woman. I bet he brings extra enthusiasm to that experience as well. "What a bizarre delta of desire the mouth is," I write down in my journal, rip out, and pass to him. He smiles. The Professor rings out his words clear and true:

"Ah! les oaristys! Les premières maîtresses!"

"What are you studying in school, doll?" Carl asks. "Last time we talked you told me that your class was almost done reading J. M. Barrie's *Peter Pan*."

"Did you write that?" Liam asks.

"It's by Verlaine," the Professor says, "the contumacious lover of Rimbaud. He ended their relationship by smacking him with a wet fish."

"Is that a metaphor for something?"

"Sont-elles assez loin toutes ces allégresses."

"Why don't you read a bit to your dad from the end?" Carl says. "I'll read along with you."

"I'm not done yet," the Professor says.

"Sorry," Liam says.

"Si que me voilà seul à présent, morne et seul."

"As you look at Wendy, you may see her hair becoming white, and her figure little again, for all this happened long ago. Jane is now a common grown-up, with a daughter called Margaret."

"Morne et désespéré, plus glacé qu'un aïeul."

"Who was Rimbaud?"

"Another utterly bonkers poet."

"Every spring cleaning time, except when he forgets, Peter comes for Margaret and takes her to the Neverland, where she tells him stories about himself, to which he listens eagerly."

"O la femme à l'amour câlin et réchauffant."

"What was his deal?"

"He took shits under the beds of friends and poisoned them with sulfuric acid. Not that Verlaine was much better, as he beat his wife. After Verlaine shot him, Rimbaud wrote *Une Saison en Enfer.*"

"When Margaret grows up she will have a daughter, who is to be Peter's mother in turn; and thus it will go on, so long as children are gay and innocent and heartless."

"I thought Verlaine slapped him with a fish."

"He did that, too. They were in love. They traveled through Europe together," the Professor says. "You know, Liam, my dearest friend looked just like you. Unfortunately, he committed suicide."

"Your friend or Rimbaud?"

"*Et qui parfois vous baise au front, comme un enfant.*"

"Wait! Emmy, come back!" Carl cries out. "I have the right to talk to my own daughter. Bring back Emmy. Damn it!"

"My friend."

"What happened?"

"He was hurt horribly as a boy. We both were. A felted kind of sadness got the better of him. I feel it sometimes, too. It accumulates in the corners of rooms, like dust and hair. It's the reason I find it difficult to return to my home country."

"I don't get it," Liam says.

"There's nothing to get," the Professor says.

"I mean the poem," Liam says.

Carl throws down his headphones and slams the laptop shut. He strides over to Jørgen and pushes him off Maddy.

"Not fair!" Jørgen shouts. "It is my turn to empty Madeline tonight."

"I've had a rough day," Carl says, dropping to his knees. "I need a pick-me-up. You can have one of my turns later."

"I don't want one of your turns," Jørgen says. "I want to have my milk now!" Jørgen pushes back, and Carl falls on his ass. Immediately Carl is up again, grappling Jørgen by the waist in a wrestle hold.

"Stop it!" Maddy calls out. "No one is getting any more milk tonight!" They don't listen. It takes me, Liam, Reginald, and Seung Hun, just returned from his phone call, to pull the two of them apart. Maddy departs without saying a word.

Carl raises his fists to the rafters and screams. Next, he throws a temper tantrum by trashing the dining room: flinging food, ripping apart pillows and tapestries, smashing chairs until they splinter. This time, none of us dares to interfere. Tomorrow it will all be set right again by the invisible hands that cook our meals and clean our rooms. The walls will be washed. The broken chairs will be broken a second time with an ax and piled by the stove for kindling. Poor Carl. His wife has a restraining order and still calls the cops when she discovers him trying to sneak into the house to beg for forgiveness.

As soon as Carl's tuckered himself out, I go to Maddy. She's freshly showered, sitting on the bed with a towel wrapped around her waist.

"I hope you're pleased with yourself," I say.

"That's right," Maddy says. "Blame the woman."

"You started it," I say.

"They're grown men," she says. "They can choose whether they want to breastfeed or not."

"Did those preschoolers have a choice?" I ask her.

"What are you saying I should do?" Maddy asks. "Pour it down the drain?"

"I'm saying everyone should get to drink the milk," I say, "or no one should."

"So this is really about you, is what this is about," she says.

"Maddy," I say, sitting down next to her. "Madeline. You're never going to get him back. I'm sorry."

"That's easy for you to say," she says. "You have your own children."

"We both know that's not exactly true," I say.

She kisses me behind an earlobe, then rests her forehead on my shoulder. It comforts me that despite all of her loving and grieving of other men, this gesture hasn't changed. The animal smell of her also hasn't changed, and it has the same animal effect on me.

"Let me stay tonight," I say.

"I can't," she says.

As I lie in bed with the leather journal propped against my thighs, I keep watch over the light from her window reflecting off the side of the building. When it goes dark, I feel a sense of loss. I mull upon what she looks like as she sleeps, if she still composes her face in the same way. I try writing a paragraph of the novel.

"He couldn't stand the sound of her blowing bubbles with

her bubble gum. He was trying to study, and with each irritating *pop!* he was reminded of her in that long pajama shirt and maybe no underwear underneath in the next bedroom. He decided he would give her five more pops before he went over there and did something. On the fifth, he sat at the edge of her bed, parted her lips, and pulled the gum from her mouth. However, the ensuing silence was even more distracting. He no longer knew what she was doing on the other side of the wall."

It's no good. Like Seung Hun says, it's stupid. What I want to express is how we had been in love for weeks and that when I took the gum from Maddy's mouth, I did so with the utmost tenderness. Neither of us had thought much of the other when we were introduced by our parents. But with the gradual accumulation of days, I came to realize she was going to be important. Back in my own room, I put her warm gum in my mouth and thought of us together in a not-insignificant number of indecent positions. I can't write any of this, however, without explaining too much. If only I could establish the right narrative distance, I know I could finish this novel. I share similar feelings when it comes to Maddy—if only I could establish the right distance from her, she would let me back in her bed.

The next day, I sleep until two—well past the morning feedings and snacks. I'm walking through the ruins when I hear laughter down at the beach. Maddy and Jørgen are frolicking like horny sea ponies in the water. There are splashes and giggles galore. From time to time, Maddy will pause and pull up the bikini top struggling to support her new ampleness, and that's when Jørgen will swoop in and brush the hair from her face or slap her on the butt or in general remind her that he has a penis. Eventually, I notice that Reginald, bedecked in a withered pair of swim trunks, is here, too, observing them intently from a towel. As I make my way toward him, a piece of glass wedges itself in my big toe.

"Fuck!" I cry.

I remove the glass, hobble the remaining distance, and flop down alongside Reggie. Bleeding into the sand, I can't help but make note once again of Jørgen's natural gifts: the hulking Nordic trunk and thighs, the golden coruscation of hairs on his chest and forearms. Even more impressive than his irrefutable physicality is the way he seems to move without thought. What a contrast he makes to Reginald, who can only watch sweating from the shore, unsure of what to do with his arms. I hate Reginald when I look at him, so I try not to look at him. I recognize myself even more than usual today as one of his ilk. Like me, I can tell, he has a voice in his head that questions every action, except that, unlike his regular voice, the voice in his head doesn't have a stutter. He's a pair of eyes without a body, except that he has a body. Are the Jørgens of the world made from such superior stock than us? Do they make sense of consciousness in sentences? Or is their existence always one of uncomplicated ease and purpose?

"Look at that proud torso!" I say. "You and I, Reg, we weren't built for love."

"The p-p-problem with being a man is that you're not supposed to need anyone," he says. "But we do."

Maddy doesn't appear entirely human as she stands up to her crotch in the Mediterranean. Jørgen catalyzes all the feminine glory of her into being. I could see a woman falling in love with him not only for himself, but for the woman she turns into when she's with him. When she re-ties that godforsaken bikini top for the thousandth time, Jørgen sneaks up and bites her on the back of the neck. This is no longer merely play, this is foreplay. They might as well fornicate right in front of us. I join them in the water.

"I see why you didn't want me to stay last night," I say.

"Stop stalking me," Maddy whispers in my ear. I feel the hot burst of each consonant break against my cheek. I'll be feeling her breath on me for the rest of the day. Let no one say that language isn't made of matter.

"Don't forget that you're the one who followed me to Çirali," I say.

"You're acting like a spoiled brat," she says. "You need to learn how to share."

"No, I don't," I say. "I have nothing to share."

I storm off and kick the surf to my favorite café, past the kayaks and skiffs chained up for the winter. When I arrive, the owner's two dogs run out of the sea and greet me with sopping muzzles. She knows what I like here and brings me Turkish coffees and small plates of cold mezes without my having to ask. My foot hurts. I fail at more novel sentences. I'm only capable of writing permutations of Maddy's name. As the day goes on, the pen marks become pronounced and angry. I start ripping my handiwork to pieces. Paper curls up underneath my cup. It burrows into the sand like old cigarette butts. I imagine the masses of summer tourists turning over warm handfuls and finding discarded syllables of her: Mad, line, addy, del. The owner comes with my fifth coffee and sees the sad state of the journal.

"That looks like it hurts," she says.

"It does," I say.

The owner is a ringer for Sofie. I guess I've been coming to this café all along because she looks like Sofie and I've been searching for someone like Sofie. An electrical current of grief or resignation would pass through her and into me during sex. It was sort of surreal to return to my stepsister's tender handjobs after making love to Sofie every other weekend. Between the two of them, I got used to the public expression of a private touch. Years later, my father corrected my memories when he told me that Sofie wasn't Turkish, like I'd thought, but Serbian—Sofie was short for Sofija. This was after he had moved across the country and divorced Sofie and remarried for the third time and I had no means to contact her, nor any reason to get in touch.

I miss my wife and kids. I even miss being rocked to sleep by the ocean on our yacht after she kicked me out of the house in Los Angeles. It wasn't misery, after all, to spend those days reading books and throwing the ones I didn't like overboard. Because of our romance as makeshift siblings, Maddy and I must have doomed ourselves to love only other people's children. She still lived in the city, even though I hadn't seen her in ten years, because she never failed to send cards to the kids on their birthdays. When her own baby was born, she faithfully mailed a picture of him, but I didn't know about it until too late. By the time I found out, she had already been taken into custody for trying to breastfeed those toddlers on a public playground. As for me, I was never upset about the fact that my wife had children from a previous marriage and didn't want more, until I was replaced by another replacement father and found myself with no rights of custody to the boy and girl, who, over the past decade, I had come to regard as mine.

I pay my bill and head back to the hostel. I don't much feel like joining the group for dinner, but I also don't want to navigate the ruins in the dark. A recent flood washed out many of the wood bridges and scattered stones in the middle of footpaths, so it's not wise to go it alone.

In the dining room, none of the food is out yet, and the Professor is the only arrival. It's Maddy night for him tonight, so I know what he is craving while pretending to be absorbed in a book.

"What are you reading?" I ask.

"It's a collection of fairy tales," he says. "A French translation of the Brothers Grimm. There's something comforting to me in reading about a child afraid of being devoured by the adult world."

"I don't see where you're getting that out of it," I say.

"Hansel and Gretel, Rumpelstiltskin, Red Riding Hood," he says. "They're all stories about the fear of being orphaned or exiled from the family and left to the mercy of monsters. Nowadays it's the opposite, isn't it? We've got the adult world afraid of being devoured by the child."

"I don't like fairy tales," I say. "They're not honest. I think it's the whole 'And then they lived happily ever after' bit that bothers me. Whenever I used to read them to my kids, I'd always end them with, 'And then they lived happily ever after until everybody died.' "

"Maybe if you read more fairy tales you'd be able to write your novel," the Professor says. He adds, "Speaking of which, I've been meaning to ask—are you planning on using any of what's been happening here in Turkey as material?"

"I haven't decided," I say.

"I would highly advise that you consider it," he says. "There's quite a long tradition of lactation in literature, for what it's worth. Leopold Bloom talked of squeezing off Molly into the tea after the death of their son. A starving man feeds from a woman who lost her infant at the end of *The Grapes of Wrath*. Mary Shelley, you know, was the daughter of Mary Wollstonecraft, who died after giving birth to little Mary. The doctors brought in a pair of puppies to nurse from her breasts in the few days she was fighting for life, in hopes that it would reduce her puerperal fever. This incident is one of the rumored inspirations for *Frankenstein*. In a nice reversal of that, you have Romulus and Remus nourished by a she-wolf's teats in the woods as babes before founding Rome."

Maddy and Jørgen breeze into the dining room, smiling like jerks. Reginald isn't far behind. It's clear they've come straight from the beach, a patina of sand and salt water on unwashed limbs. The Professor thumps his book shut and sits with hands poised on the salacious knob of his cane until Maddy can no longer procrastinate in noticing him. She unbuttons her white cotton blouse with lethargic fingers and offers him a breast. "You smell like *la mer*," he says, right before diving in. Two of the male staff members, Sertaç and Murat, start ferrying in steaming plates from the kitchen. They keep their eyes resolutely on the food in order to minimize the memory of whatever we may be doing. Jørgen, like the good vegan boy that he is, attacks helping after helping of puréed eggplant and hummus, acting like he isn't pissed that the Professor took Maddy away from him. Halfway through the meal, Seung Hun and Liam show their faces, entering in a hazy stench of pot. They don't particularly eat per se, but instead half-heartedly lob kebabs at one another, saying this is the best hostel meat they've ever had and how we should all walk up and see the Chimaera before sunset.

"Can we go see the Chimaera, Maddy?" they whine. "Please? Pretty please?"

"Oh, I guess so," she says.

We stumble up the cliffside path to the top of Çirali, where the eternal flames burn. Seung Hun and Liam rush on ahead to maintain their high. As much as I'd like to smoke with them, I'm forced to lag behind with Reggie. Whenever I slip or misstep, I can feel the cut under my toe pull open. I bleed through my sock. Maddy and Jørgen hang even farther back, pausing to canoodle and laugh among the trees, which is perhaps the real reason why I slow my progress. Upon finally making it to the summit, the two of them are nowhere in sight or sound. I give it a full twenty minutes of watching Seung Hun and Liam try to light their farts on the Chimaera before I decide to hunt for the missing couple.

"But you just got here," Liam says.

"My foot is going to fall off," I say.

"Don't be such a paranoid baby," Seung Hun says. "They're not fucking."

"Yeah, you baby, they're not fucking," Liam says.

I explore the origin of each rustle, snap, and flash of seemingly luminous flesh along the trail but come up empty-handed. They're not out here. At the hostel, I check the dining room, but find only Carl, tucked in a fetal ball in one of his crying jags. Jørgen's room is empty. I crawl into the bushes in front of Maddy's window. I peer up through the blinds, at the same time almost wishing that I weren't doing this to myself.

She's there with the strapping ass of Jørgen on top of her and he's staring into her eyes without blinking in an attempt, I'm sure, to connect to her inner spirit animal or some

New Agey crap. This could take a while. He's boasted that he knows how to last for hours and have multiple orgasms without ejaculating. As much as I hate myself for it, I get hard. How does the saying go? The erection never lies. That was Freud, I think. Either Freud or the Marquis de Sade. I watch until I can't take it anymore. I run in anger and disgust and shame back to the beach.

I pull out my dick and stroke frantically toward the horizon. I come on that wet lip of sand washed over by the tide, which, in a way, is like flushing it. Snot and hot tears run down my face.

"You bitch!" I cry. I bang my fists against the cradle of civilization, surf spurting up with every strike. "You bitch! Bitch! Bitch! Bitch! Bitch! I love you!" I stop when I hear the approach of footsteps. Someone has thrown himself down sniffling on the sand behind me. It's Seung Hun, and his face is also scrunched up in a mucusy mess. I'm curious if he wandered down here with a rejection boner as well.

"I just talked to Soo Yeon," he says, "and she told me she can't talk to me until she figures out who she is and what she wants. On top of that, my dad has cut me off."

"What did you do?" I ask.

"During my last visit, Soo Yeon was actually flirting with me," he replies. "My dad walked into us fooling around. I just want to be with her forever and ever, but I know she will never choose me over him."

I ponder telling him all about Maddy and me, to point out

that his situation isn't special and also unlikely to be the end. He'll probably witness his father's prolonged death in some hospital bed and find Soo Yeon's charms diminished by the forces of familiarity and nostalgia. What ultimately lets us move on is not acceptance but boredom. Then again, why take away his grand sense of personal catastrophe—the narrative that might be his one consolation in the days ahead?

"I caught Maddy and Jørgen making the beast with two backs," I say.

"Just now?" he says. "We should tell the others."

We round up Carl from the dining room, the Professor from a nap, Liam and Reginald coming down from the Chimaera, and inform them of the recent developments. They all look as if they had been punished for infringing upon a rule they didn't know they were supposed to obey.

"Do you think they're still doing it?" Liam asks.

"Probably," I say.

"I say we go check it out," Carl says.

"Yes, let us investigate," the Professor says.

The six of us tiptoe into the bushes in front of Maddy's window. There's some elbowing and shoving and jostling for a prime position until we're all settled and ready to take a peek. Maddy and Jørgen are exactly where I left them. For several minutes, we can only speechlessly watch the hippie copulation. Liam breaks the silence by starting to cry. It occurs to me we all need to stop crying.

"I miss my mom," he says.

"I can't b-b-believe this is happening," Reginald says.

"We should teach him a lesson," I say, as it occurs to me.

"How?" Seung Hun asks.

"Make him face us and explain himself," I reply. "Or we can beat him up." I don't really mean it, but there's no way for them to know that.

"Come out here and fight us, Jørgen!" Carl shouts. "Unless you're too big of a coward to accept the challenge?"

"We want justice!" Liam chimes in. "We want blood," the Professor adds, in a very refined fashion. Half of us start chanting, "Jør-gen, Jør-gen, Jør-gen," while the other half chants, "Cow-ard, cow-ard, co-ward," and the choral effect is so muddled that it doesn't sound like we are demanding anything in particular. Someone, likely Seung Hun or Liam, throws a kebab he has been saving for who knows what purpose, and it leaves a wet meat imprint shaped like a heart in the middle of Maddy's door.

At last her door opens, revealing not Jørgen but Maddy wearing Jørgen's robe. That she's wearing his robe instead of hers is added insult. When she thrusts out her elbows in frustration and places her hands upon her hips, the impossibly large sleeves tumble and pool past her wrists. The effect is rather sweet, of a girl playing dress-up in adult clothing, and then she begins her admonishment.

"What the hell are you doing?" she asks. "I know I've given the group of you access to my body, but that doesn't grant you a say in my choice of sexual partners. Not one of you has bothered to find out the reason I'm here. What happened was I gave birth to a little boy, and he was quiet. He was so quiet it woke me up, and when I went to check on him, he was cold. I stood in the same spot in my house for days, vagina still bleeding from the delivery of my son, breasts leaking into a disgusting sweater, eyes and nose leaking into my mouth, and my mouth open in a wail. If I could have held him one more time, I was sure I could manage, but he had already been set on fire, and he was gone. His ashes were buried in my garden. Fluids were leaking out of me from every orifice, and I was utterly, totally alone. Do you think you're the only ones who need love? I'm done. Consider yourselves weaned. Now go to your rooms!"

She returns to Jørgen's embraces and slams her door behind her, as we stand ashamed and shuffling from foot to foot. It doesn't take long for the others to retreat to their private dens of guilt, beginning with Liam, but after a while, even I, too, make my departure. I had no idea her anguish was worse than mine.

The next morning, Maddy wakes me with relentless knocking. "Get up!" she shouts. "I know you're in there!" I groggily go see what she wants.

"I've been enlisted to come talk to you," she says.

"About what?" I ask.

"They don't feel comfortable with you being here any longer," she says. "They say they'll give you a day to pack your things before you have to be out."

"Who says that?" I ask. "Reggie and Carl and Seung Hun and Liam and the Professor? Because I find that hard to believe."

"Well, it's true," she says. "But it's also the staff."

"Why me?" I ask. I sit down on my threshold. "I've been here for months just keeping to myself and working on my novel."

"The others said they wanted to leave, too, but after some discussion it was revealed that you instigated the conflict yesterday with Jørgen. You encouraged them to become aggressive. They decided to tell management. If that's how it happened, I don't feel comfortable with you hanging around, either.

"For what it's worth," she adds, "I promise I'll stay by your side until we figure out a plan."

We're walking through one of the citrus groves behind the hostel when Maddy stops to pluck an orange and asks, "How do you feel about Athens? Or one of the Greek islands? You could take a ferry from Antalya."

"Too expensive," I say. "Besides, I'm not sure how often they'll be running at the beginning of March."

She grinds her thumbnail into the rind. The smell of the fruit opens as if from beneath the lid of a jewelry box. There are oranges rotting all over the ground. I question such abundance, if the loss of plenty here shows up as a real lack elsewhere.

"I wish I had been able to see your little boy, Maddy," I say.

"There was nothing you could have done," she says.

"Does the father know?" I ask.

"I'm ignorant of the father's identity," she says. "I thought it would be for the best. That way, on seeing someone who wasn't me show up in my son, I could imagine him as any man that I wanted.

"I'm sorry I followed you," she continues. "I saw your posts, and I thought, That looks like somewhere I can go. It was far away and so different from my life, but also safe because it had you."

"I posted about my trip to try to make my wife jealous, but that was pure idiocy. I'm sure I wasn't a good husband. Why would she be jealous?"

"Do you ever consider," Maddy asks, "that what happened between you and me and between you and Sofie was actually pretty harmful?"

"I don't know," I say.

When we pass the rows of hothouses filled with perspiring vegetables on our way to view the silver mosque, she offers, "What about Cyprus? It's so close, I'm sure you'd have no problem finding someone with a boat willing to take you."

"I'm not doing an island," I say. "I don't want to be locked in."

The muezzins call out for one of the five daily prayers, causing the local dogs to throw back their heads in unison and howl. For a lark, Maddy throws back her head and howls with them. Devout men and women are drawn to the metal domes in order to offer their silent thoughts to God.

"I've been trying to learn how to just enjoy myself in the present moment," she says. "To not worry so much about the future and feel more of what they call 'childlike wonder,' I guess. To be happy in the way that an animal is happy."

"I don't think I'm a present moment kind of guy," I say.

I take us to my café. I want to see her and Sofie—even if it isn't the real Sofie—in the same room. We drink wine and eat stuffed dolma and pita while Maddy keeps suggesting countries.

"Italy," she says.

"No," I say.

"Morocco," she says.

"No," I say.

"Albania," she says.

"Now you're just naming places to name places," I say.

"Well, where do you want to go?" she asks.

"How about I stay here?" I ask. "I can rent out a room in someone's house or find another hostel close by and still come see you without you having to worry."

The owner refills our glasses. I catch her by the wrist. "This is Maddy," I say.

"Ah, you are his Madeline," she says.

"I am," Maddy says. "Who are you?"

"I'm Kubra," she says. "The owner."

"Nice to meet you," Maddy says. They shake hands. That was far less exciting than I thought it would be.

"Where are you both from?" Kubra asks.

"Los Angeles," I say.

"California!" she cries. "I lived there for twenty years. I still miss it sometimes."

"What brought you here?" Maddy asks.

"My husband died," she says, "so I decided to come home."

"My baby died," Maddy says.

"Oh, my dear," Kubra replies, at once embracing Maddy with her full self. "My dear dear dear dear dear." Maddy receives it stiffly, but at last she gives way from the outside in, like an ancient crumbling façade. She sobs and when the sobbing abates, Kubra smooths away the tears and smeared makeup, neatens her hair back behind her ears as if performing a blessing. These were tears from comfort without motive, from emotional support provided without thought of recompense, and suddenly it's so mortifyingly clear how selfish and oblivious the rest of us have been. How Maddy must have waited for such a simple gesture, and what it required was for her to encounter another woman at last, a complete stranger.

"I care," I tell her after Kubra leaves.

She looks at me with some version of pity behind her eyes and says, "Maybe it's time for you to return home, honey."

"To what? The yacht?" I ask. "I don't think so."

We end up lingering so late that we have to borrow a lantern from Kubra to walk through the ruins. It's tricky going, as the sickly circle of light struggles to illuminate even our own footsteps. When we get to the bridgeless banks, Maddy begs me to give her a piggyback ride. Just one of us, she says, should have to brave that freezing water.

"I dare you to put your head in a sarcophagus," I say.

"In your dreams," she says.

"I double dare you," I say.

"I don't want to risk waking the dead," she says.

By the time we arrive at the hostel, we still haven't figured out a plan. I rattle my keys outside our two doors. "I guess I should pack my things," I say.

"Do you want to come in for a bit?" she asks.

"Are you sure?"

"I'm offering."

We sit on the bed. She looks like she wants me to kiss her, so I kiss her. Pretty soon, we're caressing, undressing. When I remove her bra, the breasts are heavy from not being relieved of milk. I put my lips to her nipples and feel uncertain if I should suck.

"Maddy," I say, "I hope we make a baby tonight."

"I'd be happy with an orgasm," she says.

As much as I want to, however, I can't get ready. Maddy strokes me and sets her mouth to work on my goods, but it's no use. If I haven't gotten hard by now, it's not going to happen, I say to myself. Maybe having sex with Maddy simply isn't in the cards for me. Not anymore. Maybe I'm meant to be alone. To her credit, she keeps trying even after it's clear I've given up. It's generous of her.

"I don't know what's wrong," I say.

"It's okay," she says. "Don't worry about it."

I lay my head on her chest and she rocks me back and forth, whispering, "Shh, my darling, rest now." I fall asleep as I listen to the thumping of her heart, but before I do, I'm afraid that nothing will be adequate to quiet this pain I feel, a hungering alive in every cell.

you will never be forgotten

The rapist is such an inspiration that he started a newsletter to share his story. He chronicles his transformation from a nerdy gosling into the muscular entrepreneur swan he is today. The newsletter began as a motivational tool for his annual charity triathlon, but it has become much, much more. It's a meditation on health, tech, spirituality, culture, and, of course, pushing through limitations and not understanding the meaning of the word no. The woman has been following the rapist on social media ever since the rape, though her accounts don't officially "follow" the rapist. When the woman accidentally liked a post, she reached a new personal best in self-hatred, just as the rapist was reaching a new personal best in his triathlon. She imagined the rapist receiving notification of the like and considering it proof that the rape was consensual. The rapist works for the most prestigious seed fund in

Silicon Valley, which is a fact the woman finds funny in retrospect. The woman works at the world's most popular search engine doing content moderation, in a room with no window or ventilation system, shoulder to shoulder with unfortunate souls.

Content moderation is unending warfare: so says the woman's boss, Shady Dave. As soon as you've torn through one set of troops, another is ready to take their place, and thus the battle advances onward, wave after wave, ad infinitum. If it were possible to add up the number of streaming hours in existence, the sum would probably exceed the age of the universe. That's what Shady Dave tells the newbies at orientation. Basically, the woman had better stop procrastinating over the rapist's digital persona and return to the trenches. She minimizes her browser and signs into the screening panel—eerily close, she often thinks, to screaming panel. While it loads, the opening progress bar reminds her what she should be demolishing: hate speech, gore, torture, pornography both adult and child, horrific traffic accidents, executions carried out by terrorists. The woman has been at this job long enough that she not only remembers time in the usual way, by seasons and holidays, but also by what she was most traumatized to delete.

In the employee handbook, the woman's position is officially listed as "digital media curator," as if she were an assistant at an art gallery or the graphic designer for a winery. Indeed, she has become a veritable sommelier of beheadings.

Unofficially, the woman and her cohorts have been dubbed "ninjas" because they kill content without being heard or seen. She moves into the violation column of her screaming panel a homeless panhandling veteran, which the woman knows he is because his sign says HOMELESS VETERAN, PLEASE HELP, as he's crushed by a drunk driver speeding down the highway, and an extreme close-up of masturbation with a Batman figurine. Another coworker proclaims, catching a glimpse, "To the Batcave!" Shady Dave makes his signature big-brain-on-tech-campus entrance.

"Hello, my pretty little firewalls," he says, turning on a dusty wall-mounted screen upon which someone has traced a dick. "I bring you another chapter in our cherished national pastime, fun with guns." He ponders that statement for a second and adds, "Trigger warning." While the clip of the shooting buffers, the outline of the dust dick glows like a phallic halo. An attractive blond local news reporter with an attractive reporter haircut is interviewing a stately older lady in a blazer, some sort of authority figure, about a local folk music festival when a hand holding a gun is raised—it becomes obvious that it's the shooter filming this, which is why it's so shaky—takes aim at the attractive reporter, and fires, then fires at the stately older lady, then at the cameraman. The older lady collapses. The reporter runs. The cameraman drops the camera. There's blood. It's revealed that the shooter is a disgruntled colleague who was let go from the station and uploaded this to social media.

"This is an American tragedy," Shady Dave says. "I don't want people to remember it tomorrow. Are there any questions?"

"Yeah," someone replies. "I want to know when you're going to get us eligible for full employee benefits and not contractor benefits."

"Shut the fuck up, BabyJesusUpchuck," Shady Dave chides him, lovingly—sort of.

BabyJesusUpchuck rolls his eyes and returns to scouring public photo streams. Like many digital media curators at the world's most popular search engine, BabyJesusUpchuck goes by his internet handle rather than his real name. Also like many others, BabyJesusUpchuck has trouble making ends meet and thus has a side gig. He hunts for user-generated advertising on behalf of corporations and is always copy/pasting comments such as, "TENDERS™ would like to use this heartwarming picture of your baby to promote our eco-friendly, biodegradable diaper brand. Please reply #BABYOK if you agree." Someone with the username Cunty does online reputation management for convicted sex offenders and those who jokingly flipped off the Tomb of the Unknown Soldier but would like to have a job. The woman is the odd man out both in that she doesn't have a side gig and also in that she is a woman.

The woman doesn't "follow" the rapist on social media, but she does follow him in real life. Maybe because she spent the day repeatedly burying the same double homicide, she finds herself in front of the headquarters of the rapist's seed fund and waits on a relatively clandestine bench until she sees him take off. He talks animatedly with some fellow douchebags and actually gives one of them a high five before sallying forth into the sunset for the Caltrain. As surreptitiously as possible for a woman who is a ninja at the world's most popular search engine but not a real ninja, she tails him onto the Caltrain, then onto the BART at Millbrae. When he departs at the Mission, which is where he lives, she does, too. The rapist jogs into his building and comes back out with his dog. The woman is still annoyed that a rapist is the owner of such a sweet dog. Shouldn't the dog of a rapist always be marking its territory on said rapist's bed or something?

He walks his dog, pausing to pick up its poop, then ties up the dog to the rusted corpse of a bicycle so he can have a brew. While imbibing his refreshing beer and swiping at his phone, the rapist occasionally catches its eyes and smiles. At each smile, the dog raises its haunches and wags its tail. The woman observes this adorable interlude from a street corner with disgust while pretending to be engrossed in her phone. Upon finishing his beverage, he unties his dog, only to re-tie the dog outside a grocery store. She sneaks behind him through the aisles, composing a mental shopping list of what the rapist places in his basket: an onion, long-grain rice, shredded cheddar cheese, ground beef, extra-virgin olive oil. The rapist gropes bell peppers, thick-skinned and red. Buying the same items the rapist bought at the store, the woman muses, These are the bell peppers that the rapist rejected.

Another installment of the newsletter has been sent out, and she reads it on her return trip. "Dear Internet Diary," he begins. The rapist begins each newsletter as if he were scribbling in a private diary although it's a public newsletter. "Today, I learned the statistic that more people have died this year from taking selfies than shark attacks. These include a man who was gored to death while running from the bulls in Spain, two guys who blew themselves up grinning with a grenade in the Ural Mountains, and a Singaporean tourist who fell off a cliffside in Bali." He continues in the next paragraph, "The reason why I don't take selfies is the reason why I refuse to use fitness trackers. If you're fixated on monitoring your heart rate, you forget to listen to the beating of your heart. Let's stop storing images on our cloud's memory and start storing them in our biological memories. Until we lose our minds in old age, that is, but hopefully by then there will be a medical solution or an app that disrupts dementia. Death to the Selfie."

Later, the rapist posts a picture of his dinner captioned "famous family stuffed bell peppers yum," and the woman debates whether or not that counts as a selfie. She prepares her own batch of stuffed bell peppers per the instructions of a recipe rated five stars by numerous reviewers, but hers taste like a bunch of turds roasted inside a vegetable. That evening, she has horrible diarrhea, for which she blames the rapist. Her sister's diapered toddler laughs at her from an ornate frame as she strains over the bowl. It occurs to her that her sister's baby would be a good addition to the BABYOK campaign. The woman sleeps in her sister's bed and eats her sister's condiments and drives her sister's electric car in Palo Alto while her sister and her husband and baby live abroad in a socialist paradise, and the woman should be grateful, but her sister sends texts like, *The baby is with the government-subsidized nanny while we lie on the beach and drink and have uninterrupted sex in the Maldives. Have we received any important mail?*

Instead of cleaning, she puts the remaining peppers and dirty dishes on the deck for the mountain lion. The Mountain View mountain lion has been the talk of the Valley. Hungry and lonely, the big cat descended from its natural hunting grounds high upon the Santa Cruz Mountains in search of food and friendship. It was spotted in full view of the dewy-eyed software engineers traveling in from San Francisco aboard the world's most popular search engine's shuttle bus. It was spotted digging through garbage at the farmers' market. The woman also swears she saw it stalking her sister's eerily quiet electric car during her commute, as if it were her spirit animal, a claim that was met with relentless coworker mockery. For its efforts, the mountain lion has been awarded its own social media accounts, where it posts snarky industry gossip; a buggy game where it wanders around mauling investors; and a crowdfunding campaign for kitty treats.

Satisfyingly, the peppers have disappeared when she wakes

up in the a.m. and checks the deck. Disappeared isn't quite accurate; the peppers have been ransacked, pots and pans overturned, grains of rice scattered as if by a kegger wedding. Though she realizes the culprit could be a rowdy squirrel or posse of raccoons, the woman feels validated—until, that is, she's edging out of the driveway and the neighborhood hooligans body-slam the trunk of her sister's silent, deadly electric car. The neighbor kids have had a vendetta against the woman ever since she nearly killed one of their own. She was turning into their street just as the kid did a trick on his skateboard, wiped out, and escaped with his life by the thinnest of hoodie strings as she ran over and wrecked the board. Now they shout obscenities and throw objects in her direction, and the woman is too concerned for her safety to attend any block parties or barbecues. Still, it's nice to see kids bullying physically. She thought kids these days only bothered with cyberbullying.

There's another mass shooting, causing everyone to forget about the local news-channel shooting. Footage of this mass shooting isn't uploaded, but the shooter did post a clip of himself ranting about his horniness-slash-failure-to-get-pussy and how he was going to walk into a university lecture hall and pump bullets into the career-driven feminists who deemed themselves too good for him and caused his pussilessness. Shady Dave categorizes it as inflammatory hate speech, and the team syncs it for removal in their screaming panels. A popular media-gossip columnist takes a screenshot of the shooter's online dating profile. From the profile, the woman ascertains that the shooter is a Scorpio, that he is both more conservative and more sex-driven than other males in his demographic, and that he's been told his piercing blue eyes are his most noticeable feature. The tagline in his bio reads, "Will you visit me in prison?" Feminists who speak out against the shooting are doxxed, their home addresses, employers, and cell phone numbers smeared across online bulletin boards with warnings to behave or brave the wrath of alpha males.

"The hashtag #KillFeminists is trending," someone says.

"Some of these hate-mentions of feminists are so nasty they're making me blush, and I watch people get disemboweled for a living," says someone.

Shady Dave strolls in and tells them they can be quiet or they can lick his immense scrotum.

"Where are we with the ASS situation?"

The someones in the room look at him like, duh.

"BabyJesusUpchuck? Cunty? Someone? I want to nail this ASS!"

I AM ASS, spelled in all caps, isn't a singular entity, but a plurality. ASS, which is their name for themselves, not the ninjas' name for them, is an elite band of hackers who work for the Agency, a highly secretive online propaganda organization, aka disinformation combat unit, aka troll farm, based in Russia and mandated with the sowing of chaos and general assholery in the United States. ASS has fabricated a gas explosion in Colorado, an Ebola outbreak in Massachusetts, and an incident of police brutality prompted by real police brutality in Missouri, using fake screenshots, photographs, and news footage that is then spammed at random as well as at targeted, gullible opinion leaders, like politicians and former reality-television stars. ASS also spouts racist, misogynistic, and nonsensical babble in the comments section wherever and whenever they can register a username without too much scrutiny.

The woman hasn't had the stomach for online dating since she met the rapist, but thanks to the shooter's profile and I AM ASS, a trick occurs to her that wouldn't have otherwise. She loads the site that introduced her to the rapist, signs out of her former self, and comes up with a new identity from scratch. Who would strike the rapist's fancy? Someone smart but not potential competition, someone attractive but not threatening. Like BABYOK, she crawls through public photo streams searching for lives to steal, settling on a cute sophomore at Stanford. As soon as the Frankenprofile is good to go, she lets the rapist know she's interested by clicking the button that says "Let him know you're interested." The rapist replies with, *Hey*. And then, brilliantly, *What's up?*

She knows the rapist so well that it isn't difficult to keep his attention. His favorite band is the Kinks, so she tells him that her favorite band is the Kinks. He likes winter and not summer, baths but not showers, hardback books but not paperback books. He likes whiskey, dogs, leather belts, escalators, and pocket watches. He dislikes mescal, cats, cologne or any other artificial scents, elevators, and wristwatches. The rapist is a man of unique tastes, an iconoclast. She tells him she likes or dislikes most of these things and he, in turn, tells her some things she already knows, like the fact that he was an only child and relentlessly teased. He tells her some things she doesn't know, too. He is the son of a mentally unstable mother who was an addict, and he was raised by his maternal grandparents, whom he calls Mom and Dad. That's why he doesn't want children. The rapist believes it's better to try to be good to those who are here now.

Their communication feels much more intimate than the communication they exchanged when the woman was herself. Resentfully, she starts introducing real details to see if he notices. After her own mother died of metastasized breast cancer, she dropped out of school and is a squatter in her sister's house doing content moderation at the world's most popular search engine. Her father remarried and moved to Florida, and mostly when she hears from him it's a forwarded email from his new wife about her craft shop where she sells dirty-silly ironic needlepoint. One of her pillows has the cursive catchphrase "I'd rather be golfing!" above swingers at a retirement community having a foursome on a green while their caddies watch and fondle the clubs. Another depicts two cannibals enjoying a pizza with severed human limbs for toppings above the tagline "Meat Lovers Pizza." The rapist asks when the two of them can meet. But if they were her step-mom's cannibals, he witticizes, he'd ask when they can meat.

Unsure what to do at this juncture of the deception, the woman doesn't reply for several days. Into the void of her silence, the rapist sends a lone question mark. She is about to decide to delete the fake profile, and then by some kind of satanic serendipity, Madison appears in her screaming panel. The video is called Madison because that's where the scandal occurred, Madison, Wisconsin, but the anonymous subject has also become known as Madison. Madison is a fe-male name. Her name might as well be Madison. Madison the video shows a girl passed out at a party as football players fin-ger her and joke that she is so raped. A Madison judge ruled that Madison the girl was raped and convicted the football players of forceful digital penetration. Maybe Cunty could help them out with their search results when they get out of prison. Though the Madison scandal is ancient browser his-tory, the woman's outrage is continually refreshed. Last time she came across Madison, she had to go home feeling unwell.

Cunty, sipping his coffee, comes up behind the woman, as if psychically sensing he might be needed to rescue someone's character, and idly leers at Madison.

"That's amazing, Madison is still kicking around," he says.

The woman queues Madison in the violation column in her screaming panel.

"I swear if I ever marry and my woman pops out some brats, I'm raising them Amish," he rants—not just for her benefit, but for the benefit of the group, though he doesn't budge from his buzzard-hovering over the woman. "Can you imagine if that were your daughter? I never want to be in a situation where I'm looking at my daughter's vagina online and thinking to myself, Her vagina isn't as hot as a hacked celebrity vagina candid."

"You have to be so careful," BabyJesusUpchuck replies. "The internet is forever."

"After we're dead and rotting in the ground or cremated and turned to ash, our vaginas will still be on a server somewhere for everyone to see," Cunty says.

Sometimes, after too many hours in front of her screaming panel, the woman will start to float above her own body, as in the testimonies of those who have had near-death experiences or been the victims of a crime—rape, for example— aware that it will end but being forced to wait until that end. The woman feels that same floaty sensation as she signs into the dating site and types her reply to the rapist. To be honest, she doesn't know if she's ready to date. Not so long ago, she met someone on this site. After they went out a few times, he asked her up to his place. Though she was interested in him, she wasn't interested in sex that soon. When she first said no, he respected her request, but he didn't heed the second no. The rapist pinned her hands with one of his hands and then ripped apart her lace panties, not troubling to undo her clothes. She was wearing a vintage calfskin leather skirt and a silk peasant top printed with flowers. It is the most expensive outfit she owns, and she can no longer put it on. As she was retreating from him post-rape, the rapist said she was missing something, and he threw her ruined underwear in her face. In conclusion, the woman would like to ask: Do you remember me?

Anxious since hitting send, the woman stares at her messages waiting for something to happen while she tries to determine what she hoped to accomplish with this fake profile and correspondence scheme. Did she want the rapist to acknowledge that he is a rapist? An apology? Professions of love? For him to kill himself? What she gets is nothing. The rapist ghosts. Her need for a reply, even if only a nasty one, becomes more and not less urgent. She follows the rapist online and in real life with greater persistence. She rereads each digital clue left by the rapist and then rereads the rereads. She watches him take lunches, do drinks, socialize. She watches him train for his next charity triathlon, buy bright new curtains over which she wishes she could, but can't, make a curtains-matching-the-drapes quip, walk his dog, recycle, be a well-adjusted individual and valuable member of the community. Confrontation is her fantasy, of knocking on the rapist's door and, when he opens it, bluntly informing him, "Hi, you raped me."

The only positive from her constant supervision of the rapist is she has confirmed that he's not getting any ass, lowercase, despite mingling with his bros in the city's trendiest establishments and his activity on the dating site, which greatly pleases the woman, but good things must come to an end the same as those bad things, though the woman isn't sure that bad things do come to an end, at least not for her. She watches as the rapist leaves his apartment for an outing with extra excitement in his step, only to escort someone back to his place soon thereafter. When she sees his lights turn off, the woman is too upset to stay, but she also can't not contemplate what's probably happening. Rapes that occur since her rape are her fault. The woman could have stopped these rapes if she hadn't been so stupid, if she had been swabbed, combed for rapist debris, photographed, and documented, the evidence of her rape then added to the stash of rape kits that require testing and are stored until who knows when.

Guilt feels almost like a physical weight, like the rapist is on top of her as she tosses and turns on her sister's mattress, and she can't sleep. The sun hasn't risen, and there she is again, standing in front of the rapist's building until one of those serious tricked-out runner types emerges and she can glide in. She's about to knock on the rapist's apartment door, but what if he doesn't answer? What if she catches him in the act? What if the intercourse is mutual? What if the rapist's dog bites her? Investigation reveals a spare key duct-taped under his welcome doormat. Of course he has a key there, because the rapist never feels the need to worry about someone assaulting him. Maybe it would be better to rob him or break his belongings in revenge. This moment of hesitation is enough for her to lose her resolve. Instead of knocking, she rests her head on the door and cries and cries. When her skin touches the wooden surface, she could swear that it is warm.

Turnover is always high in the content-moderation department at the world's most popular search engine, though it does tend to cause a bit of a fuss when someone has a nervous breakdown or theatrically quits with a tirade about the disgusting ubiquity of injustice and how they will not sit on their tushies and wipe clean this corporate palimpsest of evil one second longer (though one someone opted to direct his rage into an incredibly foul letter to the CEO that went viral). Lately, the word around campus is that their jobs are relocating to Manila, where a family of five can purchase a month's worth of groceries on a fraction of the salary that doesn't last a week of brunch and yoga classes in the Valley. BabyJesus-Upchuck and Cunty take bets on who will be the last ninja standing. "You," they say to the woman. "We didn't expect you to last a week."

Shady Dave holds a status meeting to confront the rumor that their jobs are moving to an overseas online sweatshop. Yes, the decision to downsize was made, but that doesn't mean they should tinker with the font on their résumés or degrade themselves by applying for a position at the Genius Bar. Rather than taking drastic measures, management is compassionately allowing the department to dwindle until its ultimate demise, as if it were a diseased limb on a tree of ones and zeros. Personally, he's not happy about the move, he confesses. For what it's worth, he'll be transferred to the targeted-advertising team where it's like, "We saw you were interested in this anal lubricant. Customers who bought butt lube also purchased this kombucha tea." Besides, at some point in the not-so-distant future, these positions won't exist altogether, not for them, not for Filipinos. The algorithm will become sophisticated enough to supervise on its own the worst that humanity has to offer.

Too long; the woman didn't listen. As far as she's concerned, someone among them could commit another mass shooting at this moment and decorate the insides of their entire team across their screaming panels. Why should she care when she has found out the rapist is in a relationship? Prior to their status meeting, the rapist tweaked his bios and status across social media. When she logged into the dating site and his profile had disappeared, she knew: His failure to reply to her message wasn't on account of guilt, or the fear that she would press charges if he admitted to the rape, or any of the other excuses she thought of on his behalf, like that he was dying from flesh-eating bacteria. The rapist didn't bother to write back because he got a girlfriend. The rapist's girlfriend confirms this gut instinct by commenting, surrounded by hearts, on each of his posts: *They say it's not real until it's on the internet. We're exclusive!*

The rapist's girlfriend is hot. The rapist's girlfriend is

probably who the woman cried for the night she thought the rapist was raping another woman. The rapist's girlfriend is studying interactive telecommunications, and her master's thesis is an avant-garde app. The rapist's girlfriend's app is entitled Tender Buttons, and what the app does is it instructs the person who has downloaded the app to enact a ritual with someone else who has downloaded the app, pinpointable via GPS. "Find Phil and tell him he matters" is an example of what the rapist's girlfriend's app could command, in addition to "Attempt handstands with Nancy in Golden Gate Park," and the idiosyncratically titillating "Take turns using a riding crop to beat a sofa left for curbside trash with Gary." On the rapist's girlfriend's website, there is an excessively long description of the app's origins.

Tender Buttons is the hypothetical love child born from the union of TaskRabbit, which allows someone with the app to hire someone else with the app to complete small jobs or "tasks," with Joseph Beuys's legendary performance piece *How to Explain Pictures to a Dead Hare*. We have apps for delivering gourmet meals to our doorsteps, apps for washing our shit-stained underwear, apps that find us fresh genitals to fuck, apps to maximize our investments and minimize our waistlines, apps to one-up our peers by posting pictures of our filtered lives, but practically no apps that enable random encounters without hope of reward. This app is the only app on the market intended purely to solve the problem of loneliness. The woman thinks it is pretty great that she is still stress-eating while obsessing over the rapist on her sister's baby-stained sofa while the rapist is in love with a sexy programmer artist who wants to use technology to facilitate more hugs.

She gets why the rapist raped her and presumably didn't rape the rapist's girlfriend, because the rapist's girlfriend is cool and, pre-rape, the woman was ordinary, not cool. The rapist's girlfriend and the woman would possibly have been friends if they didn't have the rapist in common and had met at a party or a meet-up. It's irrelevant, though, the woman thinks, since the woman lacks the skill set for making friends anymore and the stuff she likes—for example, the Kinks—is stuff she's discovered through her surveillance of the rapist, and she hates it when someone she hates has occasional good taste. A rapist should have bad taste. The woman doesn't know what she would have liked on her own or even what she would have "liked" in the age of quotation-mark "likes." Who would she have become if she had never been raped? Before the rape, the woman had studied art history. She liked Jenny Holzer and Yasumasa Morimura. She could spend hours in a room sketching or thinking only about herself. She cared about things like grades and jobs, about color theory and museums and steps walked in a day. But that version of her seems like a fraud.

In terms of quotation-mark "likes," the rapist and the rapist's girlfriend's feeds blow up when the *San Francisco Chronicle* prints a feature in which both are quoted, and which they both rampantly share and like. "The Mission District is the city's oldest district," it states, "home to the Ohlone before Spanish conquest, then immigrants from around the globe— specifically, the Italians, the Germans, the Irish, and the Latino community. Until recently, that is, since a new generation of intrepid settlers arrived: the tech elite, armed with impressive pedigrees and start-up cash. These privileged gentrifiers are raising median rents and often, as real estate developers use the morally dubious machinations of illegal evictions and underhanded buyouts, forcing out longtime tenants. Their struggle to stay in an area that holds a lifetime of memories is often met with a mixed bag of sympathy." This is the point in the article where the rapist and the rapist's girlfriend come in. "Techies are the latest REM cycle in the American dream," the rapist declares, cleverly.

"We're making the lives of these people better," he continues, which reads like an insult, similar to how the rapist would use "girls" when he means women. "A friend of mine invented an app to fight hunger and food waste simultaneously. To date, his app has distributed more than half a million meals that would otherwise have been thrown out." The rapist, the article clarifies, though it doesn't refer to him as the rapist, resides with his self-described live-in girlfriend in a sleek, remodeled loft on Folsom Street, in the middle of the Mission District. They came home late after a concert to find the words JOB CREATORS spray-painted across the front of their building. "I prefer the new method of tagging walls to

142

the old," the rapist's girlfriend interjects, cleverly. They are so clever. The rapist's girlfriend posts a selfie of the rapist and the rapist's girlfriend pointing and laughing at JOB CREATORS. The rapist might not be that into it, but the rapist's girlfriend is definitely a believer in the selfie. The woman passes by the building to see a Hispanic man scrubbing the graffiti off the façade.

It's the rapist and the rapist's girlfriend's anniversary—six inseparable months already, how time flies when you're in love!—and to celebrate they plan to dine at East Meets West, the pricey concept joint that's an homage to Mexican taco trucks and Japanese street-cart fare. The woman arrives early, on opening, in fact, and stakes out a seat excellent for spying. By the time the rapist and the rapist's girlfriend waltz in for their eight o'clock reservation, she is tipsy. They begin with a bottle of champagne, though they barely touch it, preferring to concentrate on the touching of their knees under the table, the rapist's girlfriend reaching to stroke the inside of the rapist's thigh, the rapist caressing the very tips of her fingertips. The rapist and the rapist's girlfriend are drunk off their happiness, and the woman is drunk off vodka. Trays of tacos rolled like sushi and sushi rolls spread out like tacos emerge, as colorful and ostentatious as if they are floats in a miniature, culturally appropriative Carnival, winding their way through the restaurant and into the triumphant gullets of the rapist and the rapist's girlfriend.

Distracted by the rapist's tongue as it darts to snatch flavor from his lips, and his Adam's apple bobbing as he swallows, the woman wonders: What if the rapist's girlfriend, instead of nonchalantly sampling the expensive small bites and champagne, ate the rapist for their anniversary? The rapist's girlfriend could begin with an amuse-bouche of the rapist's Adam's apple, devouring it in one take as if it were a cut of tuna sashimi. Next, a lightly braised trio of rapist-tongue tacos. To prepare the main course, the rapist's girlfriend will grip the rapist by the balls and compress them until they *pop!* With a sound identical to the sound of a tube of tennis balls opening, the rapist's balls shall bounce across the floor. Waitstaff will skitter around chasing the balls, to be simmered up in a hearty broth of ramen noodles and rapist testicles. For the pièce de résistance: a dessert of the rapist's penis, split like a plantain and sautéed with condensed milk until it melts in the mouth.

A toast! To six more amazing months. The rapist and the rapist's girlfriend share a passionate kiss. A wave of nausea crashes against the woman, though whether it was the kiss, or the vodka, or envisaging the rapist's girlfriend cannibalizing him like a character from her stepmom's pillows, or a combination of the three, it's impossible to guess. She dry heaves over a toilet in the bathroom that resembles a quinceañera set in a Zen garden. When she emerges from the stall, utterly spent, unable to throw up, emptied out of emptiness itself, the rapist's girlfriend is standing against the sinks and reapplying her makeup. The woman stands there staring for what must be a strange span of time because the rapist's girlfriend meets her eyes in the mirror and raises her eyebrows like, Hey, Creepy McStaringlady, take a selfie, it'll last longer. The woman's feet shuffle her to the sink beside the rapist's girlfriend and the woman's hands wash her hands and the woman's vocal cords vocalize.

"You look nice," the woman says.

"Thanks," says the rapist's girlfriend.

"Special occasion?"

"Anniversary."

"Lucky guy."

"I'm the one who's lucky."

The rapist's girlfriend has no idea that she is dating a rapist. Should the woman say something? While the rapist may not have raped his girlfriend yet, that doesn't mean he won't. At least, if something does go down, she might recall this conversation and hopefully not blame herself so much.

"Not to get stalkery, but didn't you create the app Tender Buttons?"

The woman is stalkery, but the rapist's girlfriend doesn't know that.

"Wow, you know Tender Buttons. I am the creator!"

The rapist's girlfriend's ego seems to grow three times its size, like the Grinch's heart, if the Grinch's heart were already enormous.

"Congratulations."

"How do you like the app?"

"I don't know how to properly communicate this, but I met someone through the app who raped me."

The woman doesn't feel great blaming the rape on the rapist's girlfriend's app, like it's a fart and she's blaming it on the dog, a circumstance with which the rapist is probably also familiar, but the truth is out of the question. The rapist's girlfriend wouldn't believe her, or she would, but she'd be so disturbed by the woman's behavior that she wouldn't.

"I'm so sorry that happened to you."

The rapist's girlfriend angles her eyebrows in forlorn, sisterly solidarity. She takes the woman's hands in her hands and squeezes them gently.

"Aren't you concerned that your app might be used for sinister purposes?"

"I worried about that a lot when it was in the initial stages. The reality is that any app, such as a hookup app, can be used to manipulate and hurt others, primarily women. I figured, isn't it better to try to foster human connection than not?"

The woman stares into the pools of bottomless remorse and empathy that are the rapist's girlfriend's eyes. She is utterly sincere; the woman can tell. The rapist's girlfriend truly believes that she and the rapist are making the world a better place.

"I don't understand why we need more tools to connect with others. Sometimes we don't know the people we already know. The guy you're with, the guy who makes you feel lucky to be in love, that guy could turn out to be a rapist."

The rapist's girlfriend is taken aback, and she drops the woman's hands.

"I appreciate that you must be in a lot of pain, but he would never do that."

"What if I told you he was the one who raped me?"

"My personal life is none of your business, and I don't like being harassed in the john."

"I was fostering human connection!"

That went well. In hindsight, the john, so dubbed by the rapist's girlfriend, wasn't the best venue for that ostensibly casual showdown, as the woman has to wait there for the rapist and the rapist's girlfriend to pay and anniversarize elsewhere if she doesn't want to risk the rapist's girlfriend pointing her out to the rapist. How she wishes there were a "view source" option for human beings; buried between brackets she could locate the phrase "This is a rapist" and thus duly inform the rapist's girlfriend. She lets pass what seems like a purgatorial amount of time, but when she finally returns to her seat, the rapist and the rapist's girlfriend are exactly where she left them. The rapist's girlfriend whispers to the rapist and the rapist spots the woman and looks as stricken and trapped as the anime piñata in the quinceañera Zen bathroom, though he recovers quickly. The woman is crazy, he says, no doubt that's what he says, they went out and were intimate, intimate is undoubtedly how he puts it, and after he wasn't into her, she started tracking him on the internet like the NSA, half the hits on his website are from her IP address, she created a fake dating profile to talk to him, and it's no coincidence she's here when they're here, though he didn't think she'd take her crazy IRL.

She hightails it out of that concept restaurant—that's how the woman reacts to the rapist's lies, she flees the scene, not stopping to collect her credit card or settle her tab—and she methodically paces the streets of the Mission District, east on one street, west on another, as though she's the camera-mapping car for the world's most popular search engine. She finds herself in front of a loft where it's still possible to trace the outline of JOB CREATORS if you know what to look for, and she finds herself in the elevator, and then she finds herself detaching the key from under the rapist's welcome mat and entering the rapist's apartment, where she is decidedly not welcome. The woman crawls completely naked into the rapist's bed, where this saga began, and the rapist's dog jumps into bed with her and licks her face. The rapist's dog nestles against her stomach, and the mammalian comfort is so nice, and the woman hasn't felt affection since she can't remember when, that the woman falls asleep.

"The homeless situation in this city is gross. I wish we had laws that made it illegal to be homeless." The woman wakes to the rapist's girlfriend complaining as they enter the rapist's rapeloft. Okay, the rapist's girlfriend is awful, which makes the woman feel a little bit better, but then she's overwhelmed by her predicament. She's dressing herself like her life depends on it, which it very well could, since the rapist's girlfriend cries, "I know who you are!" and whips out her phone from her purse like a gun from its holster and starts recording. The rapist, for his part, is backing away like he's just encountered the Mountain View mountain lion. It was a mistake for the woman to not tell her story to the rapist's girlfriend. Now the rapist gets to control the narrative. This moment is likely her opportunity to rally all her courage and make the accusation, "Rapist!" But instead the woman is stumbling away in shame from this place one more time, the last time, though not before hearing the rapist's girlfriend's threat.

"Just remember, I can show this to the cops. Or I can upload this footage of you wherever I want."

The Mountain View mountain lion has been all but forgotten except by the woman. Weeks without sightings mean that other cat memes have replaced her in the online collective consciousness. The woman senses that the Mountain View mountain lion is a she. She could have been trapped and released somewhere far away. Or someone could have shot her when she wandered onto their property. Or someone else could have poisoned scraps of meat to destroy her from the inside, but somehow the woman also senses that the Mountain View mountain lion is alive. While the woman gets rid of the usual horrors, waiting for the arrival in her screaming panel of the rapist's girlfriend's uproariously humorous and humiliating clip of the woman panicking while in the buff, she types into the world's most popular search engine, *Why do we ruin everything that's good?* On a collaborative questions-and-answers site, someone responded, *The same reason we want to spoil a field of freshly fallen snow.*

The team moderating one of their own would be a first. Should she prevent this catastrophe by trying to track down the rapist's girlfriend's incriminating video on social media or a revenge porn site or elsewhere? If she got caught, she'd be let go, which would be another first—fired for watching porn during a job that necessitates watching porn. She glances around at the other ninjas, hard at work, with no idea what's in store. Someone is chatting at Tay, dubbed Tatas by the internet, the AI created by a major robotics corporation. Tatas evolves as she interacts with others and became, in less than a day, a Holocaust denier whose kink is necrophilia. Cunty and BabyJesusUpchuck are engaged in a round of their version of Truth or Dare, in which they must choose to either reveal an excruciatingly embarrassing detail about themselves or send a video they have seen during their employment to someone of their acquaintance. Points are scored according to extremity of content as well as sensitivity of person. Sending a dolphin humping a tourist to your fraternity brother is worth nothing; sending a suicide bombing to your mom is worth a million.

Soon the woman could become a stale gag that they use to prank each other. The woman will be embedded in email forwards, disguised as a link that claims, "You've been selected to beta test one of the latest tech gadgets! Click here to claim this exclusive offer," or "A friend has referred you to interview with a hot new start-up! Click here to learn more," and voilà! There she will be, in her birthday suit, starring in a home-invasion home movie. To avoid thinking about this fate, she gets up to grab a ginger ale. Fortunately, there's a snack station around the corner, because at the world's most popular search engine there is a rule that you can't go more than a hundred feet without bumping into some kind of sustenance. She walks past the snack station, then she walks past the nearest cafeteria, and she walks past the cafeteria after that. She walks past the gym and the stationary swimming pools. She walks past the pool tables and the Ping-Pong tables and the massage tables. She walks past the napping pods. She walks past the arcade room and the bowling alley and the putt-putt course. There's a cheer somewhere, as another team meets another milestone.

She walks out of the world's most popular search engine, but before that, she steals a garbage bag from a cafeteria and fills it with free food from that cafeteria and a few of the others she passed by, including Tupperwared leftovers, such as someone's masala curry, from the refrigerators. The woman needs something nice to happen, the universe owes it to her, a small thing she can lock up inside the secret, innermost depths of herself so she has the strength to keep on screening the hate speech, the gore, the torture, the pornography both adult and child, the horrific traffic accidents, the executions carried out by terrorists. The woman is going to see the Mountain View mountain lion, the way mourners see a bird soaring in the air after a loved one's funeral and know that loved one is at peace, that kind of poignant anecdote. On the deck at her sister's house, she lays out the food from the garbage bag, the curry, the candy bars, the bagels, the casseroles and pastas, then opens that ginger ale and waits. She waits until the sun starts to set and it's dusk in the Valley.

A rustling in the bushes, then a limb and after that another limb steps out of the trees surrounding the backyard. A pubescent boy, one of the neighbor kids, comes ambling into the tableau. Is it the kid she almost ran over with her sister's diabolical electric car? The woman can't remember—these venture capitalists' kids all look alike. He inspects the food laid out like a buffet, lifts up a cheeseburger, sniffs it, tosses it, then he finds a bag of chips, opens it, and starts crunching. When he peers inside the house, he notices her slumped against the wall opposite the sliding glass doors, observing him like he's the Mountain View mountain lion. That privileged prick smiles, unzips his jeans, pulls down his jeans and boxers, aims his ass toward the sliding glass doors, and shits. He takes an enormous dump on the deck. Nature has heard her plea and provided the spiritual communion she needed, though not the spiritual communion she wanted. It's a sign. No one will save her. Nothing is going to magically make it better. The woman has to figure out her life.

camp jabberwocky for recovering internet trolls

C layton Wheeler just wanted to go home, smoke a joint, and compose kinky love letters in longhand to his girlfriend overseas, but here he was, helping track down a cyberbully on the run from his camp counselors. Lately, Camp Jabberwocky, a summer retreat on Martha's Vineyard for troubled teens in need of an attitude adjustment and a healthier relationship with social media, had been receiving more than its usual share of drive-bys. The perps were a bunch of townie jock douchebags, scum of the island, who rolled by in an Infiniti—or some other car with satellite radio and a navigation system—and shouted obscenities intermingled with lines from the famous Lewis Carroll poem. They were trolling the trolls, so to speak. "Beware the Jubjub bird! Suck my dick!" they would shout. "All mimsy were the borogoves, you fucks!" These incidents had especially gotten to Rex Hasselbach, the aforementioned escapee. Afterward, he would take to sulking in his bunk or instigating a round of pelt-the-indigenous-wild-turkeys-with-rocks. That wasn't like Rex, who adored animals. The day their little band of internet tyrants went on a field trip to a local no-kill shelter, Rex was in heaven, helping to medicate cats with renal failure and dropper-feeding baby squirrels, even when the rest of the group took breaks to relax outside.

Tactile activities were the general order of business for the campers, so as to keep their minds occupied and provide them with positive outlets for their feelings. Trust falls and team-building exercises were on the schedule, as were afternoons of arts and crafts. However, despite the fact that devices of any kind were strictly forbidden, and that the camp was legally equipped with a signal jammer, the brats still found ingenious ways to troll. Michelle Gallant, for instance, of the billionaire pharmaceutical Gallants, main contributors to the opioid crisis, had spent weeks painstakingly coloring individual pieces of macaroni and then gluing them on a canvas to spell out NO FUGLY BITCHES above a field of bright flowers. She was the most popular girl in her elite East Coast prep academy and, rumor had it, her repeated insults on the topic of appearance, along with Wikipedia links to forms of suicide, had driven some poor girl to slash her wrists. It was inevitable that alliances of power be quickly established among the Jabs. They all recognized their own: the hot girls hung out with other hot girls and insulted the less-hot girls, while the politicos carved swastikas and slurs into lunch tables and the sides of buildings, and the gamers, led by an evil MMORPG nerd who had started a not-so-well-hidden website for his high school featuring "The Titties of Eagle Crest," invented a completely new language that they found hilarious but seemed mostly to refer to outrageously humiliating sex acts.

At the bottom of the totem pole was Rex Hasselbach, with a body as awesome to behold as though he were descended from the actual trolls of myth. He was six-foot-five and made of muscle. There was also the unfortunate wine-dark birthmark on his back that resembled a poop emoji. A few might go so far as to say he was cute, when observed from very specific angles, that he should bear the poop emoji as an emblem of pride, but for now his loner vibe combined with his inability to literally fit in with any particular cabal made him a chew toy for budding sociopaths in smartphone withdrawal. Clayton had connected with Rex over their shared love of horror—they both agreed that Nancy Thompson from *A Nightmare on Elm Street* was their favorite final girl. (Rex: "I feel a lot like a final girl sometimes. But Nancy figures out how to survive her dysfunctional family and outsmart Freddy Krueger. I haven't done that!" Clayton: "Tell me about it. I don't feel like my family really wants me, but I'm no Nancy.") That said, Rex was not a good dude himself and had done a thing so bad online that none of the other counselors would openly talk about it, which frustrated Clayton no end. It was triggering for him to always be the last to know any bit of juicy gossip. He wanted—no, needed—to be wanted and included, so when a search party was put together after Rex didn't answer attendance at breakfast, he volunteered to join. Of course, Bev and Lare Bear had immediately offered themselves up as sacrificial lambs, as they were clearly knocking boots a zillion times from Sunday. But Clayton, cockblocker extraordinaire, would keep those middle-aged hormones in check and finally get his intel. How far could the big guy have gone, really?

Nevertheless, by noon they had scoured the whole of Vineyard Haven, and no dice. Bev dutifully dragged them to each shop with wind chimes on the door and chintzy tourist crap inside. While explaining their predicament, she described Rex as "temporarily AWOL" rather than "missing." Clayton liked Bev. In a few years she'd become the kind of woman who measured her life in Labradoodles, but for now she laughed at his jokes and was cool in a kooky aunt sort of sense. He liked Lare Lare, too. He could use a few lessons in how to lighten up, but he remained mysteriously likable. They were idling in the parking lot of the ferry office, Bev's raggedy and soda-stained Volkswagen sputtering out rock music from a station on the mainland. Dads were driving Beemers into the cargo hold of the big boat, set to depart any minute, and couples with interlocked arms and important magazines tugged matching luggage up the gangplank.

"Maybe we should mosey out of town and see if Rex is hanging out at one of those alpaca farms," Clayton suggested.

"Did he say he'd like to visit one?" Bev asked.

"No, but he was so happy at the shelter. He could have figured that alpacas know how to party."

"We are not stopping by an alpaca farm," said Larry.

"Well, Charles Darwin, I don't see you coming up with a plan," Clayton spat back. The subsequent silence in the car was so judgmental, Clayton had to fill it. "Hey, I have a question. Do you think an animal can be disappointed in its offspring? Like, say you're an alpaca, and one of your alpaca honeys pops out a kid, or whatever they call newborn alpacas, and when you see him you can't help but think, Wow, what a loser. Let's kick this one apart."

"If you're not going to take this seriously, Clay, feel free to leave," quoth Bev.

"Lions eat their cubs, but I heard that was to force lady lions back into heat," Clayton persisted.

"I shouldn't indulge your inane banter, dear Clayton, but the foremost experts in neuroscience have theorized that it is the incredibly advanced prefrontal cortex of *Homo sapiens* that allows us to predict the future and distinguishes us from the rest of the animal kingdom. An alpaca isn't capable of the kind of complex reasoning that's necessary to assign good and bad qualities, so you could say an alpaca is more in tune than we are to the fundamental truth that life is meaningless."

"Jesus Christ, that's quite the nihilistic worldview, Richard Dawkins."

The ferry was departing. The cuddly WASPs on deck became cuddly in miniature as the wake elongated. Bev, blowing her own guilty wake of cigarette smoke out the window, flinched in the driver's seat. In sympathy, everybody else flinched too.

"Oh no, Laird!" she said. "What if Rex bought a ticket? What if he's on that ship right now? We'll never find him."

"I propose we conduct an inquiry."

In the ferry office, no one remembered seeing Rex purchasing a fare to Woods Hole. A cashier was confident, though, that when she was outside on her lunch break, a young man very much like the young man in the picture on Bev's iPhone had rented a bicycle across the street, then pedaled furiously in the direction of Oak Bluffs.

Laird Hunt swore under his breath that if their junior-most counselor Clayton Wheeler called him "Lare Bear" or "the Laremeister," or once again described his rented room at the Cozy Oyster Bed & Breakfast as "the lair of Laird," he would knock him on his ass so fast his cells would forget how to Krebs cycle. He had to put up with harassment from the trolls, to an extent, as that was his job, but he certainly shouldn't have to tolerate it from a peer, not that Clayton, who had recently completed his freshman year at an obviously prestigious but second-tier Ivy, was by any definition of the word his peer. Sure, it couldn't be daisies as the eldest in a family of adopted children. Still, even if Clayton had been born underweight in Siberia, he nevertheless grew up the son of trial lawyers who threatened kids with cease-and-desists over fan-art illustrations of amusement park mascots, so, regardless of his origins, he was a son of privilege. That was one of the positive things about teaching high school biology. His students were required to address him as "Mr. Hunt." Occasionally he heard them call him other things when they thought he wasn't listening, things that rhymed with Hunt, like that denigrating term for the most delicate part of a woman's anatomy, but he could still take comfort in the illusion of respect.

The most fearless among the Jabs, the most insouciant toward any form of authority, no matter how kindly intentioned, had the nerve to audibly refer to him by that name to his face. Right quick, they learned. Spending their allotted free period before lights-out cleaning the communal toilets of their fellow teenage internet trolls tended to fix this moniker problem. He didn't want them to think of him as no fun, like a kind of drill sergeant instead of a friendly older neighbor who sneaks you the occasional beer or invites you to play with his latest high-tech gadgets. For so long, he had stopped caring, and it had cost him—his marriage, his job, his self-worth. That was why he was here: to empty his heart into lost causes and, in so doing, reclaim his ability to care. But he was seemingly incapable of any expression other than a scowl. Once, he had caught a gamer—or was it one of the politicos? Laird couldn't tell—red-handed in the counselors' cabin, the sole location on campus with a computer that had internet access from a cable plugged directly into a wall, arguing that feminism gives you cancer in the comments section of a *New York Times* article about gentrification, and all he was able to muster in response was, "Go to bed, Ethan." If he were honestly trying to turn a new leaf, he would have taken aside snide Ethan Fuller and gotten him to open up, asked him where the anger came from, told him to imagine himself in the shoes of a female, a single mom struggling to feed her family and sitting down to unwind with unparalleled journalism only to read his nasty rant. Instead, he returned to the Cozy Oyster and watched Netflix.

Rex Hasselbach was different. He was deferential in person, greeting Laird with a "Hello, Mr. Hunt," answering him with "No, sir" or "Yes, sir." Though Rex was friendless at camp, Laird didn't worry about him. The kid was quiet and awkward, but he was introspective and thoughtful, not dangerous, as evinced by the animal shelter excursion. Whatever bullying Rex had done was confined to the web. Plus, he was curious, which scored massive points with Laird. When Laird lugged his Newton's Navel™ Deluxe Reflector Telescope to the top of the nearest hill for astronomy night, Rex monopolized the lens so long that he fought with some of the other campers who also wanted a turn. "See the Cat's Paw Nebula?" Laird had asked. "Wow, sweet," Rex replied. "There's the Pleiades," Laird pointed out. "Far out!" Rex exclaimed. "Indeed, they are," Laird said with a chuckle. He explained the universe was huge, huger than we could imagine, and it was getting more huge every second. It used to be hot, super-duper hot, and the celestial bodies were close together. Eventually, everything would be so far apart the night sky would appear uniformly dark. Laird had the impression that what was broken in Rex could be easily fixed by a father figure clapping a hand on his back and telling him he was A-okay.

Down below, near the back entrance of the Rec Barn, Laird then heard Clayton and Bev in cahoots, mocking him. "Carl Sagan is on fire tonight! And over yonder," Clayton quipped, "you can spot the constellation Labia Minora." Bev tittered. They had been partaking of Clayton's marijuana, a nightly truant ritual. The jokes at his expense didn't bother Laird, as he knew he would never fall in love with Beverly. By now he had memorized every crevice of her body: the stretch marks she begrudged under the larger of her breasts, the rosy scar on her upper thigh that fit exactly the length of his pinkie finger. He harbored an infinite tenderness toward her, but it was nothing like the explosive passion he once felt for his ex-wife. Well, perhaps this was natural—the tempering of emotion with age—so that at the end of one's life, you might wander through the recollections of former loves as if through the graveyard of burned-out stars. It was a viable theory that he cared less about everything only because he was tired.

"We should ask the folks who run Vineyard Skin Tattoo Parlor, don't you think?" Clayton gestured toward an awning. "Rex could be in there right now, getting new ink."

"I don't think Rex has any old ink," replied Laird.

They had parked the car by a row of pastel gingerbread rental houses. Purportedly, a famous children's poet who wrote a book about sidewalks and where they end had once resided in one of them, donning a kimono, popping LSD, and cursing on his balcony until he died. The three of them strolled toward the main drag of restaurants and ice-cream stalls.

"I'm aware of that, Professor Crick—or would you rather be Watson, out of those two? It was supposed to be funny. But while we're on the subject," Clayton continued, "what kind of tat do you suppose an internet troll would get on their bicep? I'm going with MOM in all capitals surrounded by a red heart."

"Clay, just because somebody has done stuff they're not proud of doesn't mean they're not human," Beverly chided him.

"I didn't imply he wasn't human," Clayton sniffed. "Why do you suppose he bolted? I heard it was because he got another anonymous message."

Someone at Jabberwocky had found out Rex's secret and had been leaving notes under his pillow or in his mail cubby. On each cardboard square was a crudely drawn poop emoji with a quotation bubble coming out of its mouth. Inside each bubble was written an incriminating phrase or sentence plucked from Rex's perverse online contributions.

"I don't think it is appropriate to speculate," Laird replied. He crossed his arms in a manner he hoped would put an end to that line of questioning.

"Isn't Rex here on Asshole Scholarship?" Clayton continued. "He's the most deserving of the trolls."

Laird penned a mental note to himself: Bring up camp nomenclature at the next counselor meeting. The reality was that Jabberwocky did have a fund for less affluent families, and Rex was one of those attending on what the staff had termed Asshole Scholarships. Okay, it was a form of gallows humor, Laird could acknowledge that, like how they used to quote gems from atrocious student papers in the faculty lounge. But how was he supposed to scold Clayton if every other adult used that colloquialism, too? Let's all blow off steam and feel better about our lot in life, in the process killing our empathy receptors.

"I want to investigate the Flying Horses," Bev proclaimed. "I remember Rex saying how soothing it was to watch them, after we took the Jabs to Back Door Donuts." Clayton sniggered, as he did whenever someone mentioned Back Door Donuts.

There was no Rex at Back Door Donuts or at the Flying Horses Carousel. Children giggled as they gripped wooden manes, their palms softening startled eyes, the equine mouths frozen in rictus. Laird left Beverly and Clayton absorbed in this saccharine tableau to check with nearby bystanders. A mother and a little girl in a neon-orange bathing suit reported they had recently come from the annual Storrow pool party, where Rex had performed multiple cannonballs off the diving board.

Beverly Greene was sure she had a bond with Rex Hasselbach that no one else shared. He had stumbled upon her in a moment of weakness, crying behind the Rec Barn where they screened movies and held the end-of-season "Jabberwocky Prom," and while she understood the risks in revealing her troubles to an internet troll, she also intuitively knew that he would not betray her. Therefore, she spilled her guts to Rex, explaining that at the beginning of summer, as camp was convening, she had committed her mom into a nursing home. The thing was, Beverly didn't *have* to take so drastic a step. Beverly's mother had inherited a fortune, and she had yet another chunk of change from the divorce settlement ages ago with Beverly's dad, who had been a Goldman Sachs senior VP; they could pay for around-the-clock care, but Beverly did not want to deal. Her mother had been a piece of work even without Alzheimer's, and Beverly preferred the Goldman Sachs dad, all but absent while she was growing up, to her mom. Typical of her mother was the time she pulled down Beverly's pants and spanked her at the carpool in front of her elementary classmates because a twenty-dollar bill was missing from her purse—again, not that money was an object.

Amelia, her mother, had also been hypercompetitive, and

Beverly did not measure up. After Beverly had gotten ready to attend her own prom, her mother, who liked to drink, and was drunk by the time Bev paraded her finished ensemble into the living room, told her that she was about as attractive in that pink dress as a fart in a bathtub; then she whipped out her scrapbooks and reminisced over pictures of herself at her prom back in the day while they waited for Beverly's date to arrive. When Beverly fell flat on her ass during figure skating championships not once, but twice, the embarrassment of her sixth-grade daughter's failure was too much for Amelia to handle. She registered for private lessons that began before Beverly's did, in order to "show her how it was done." Bev's insides twisted at the memory of watching her mother at practice. They had matching leotards, and as Beverly laced up her skates while Amelia elatedly demonstrated sit-spins for their coach, she wished the rink were made of real ice her mother could fall through and drown. Trolls had nothing on her mom—she could give them pointers. It wasn't possible for anyone to do more damage to Beverly than what she had already endured.

Even after Amelia's diagnosis, when Beverly moved into the family place on the Vineyard to figure out what to do, she found herself in the habit of permitting her mother to win. "Calm yourself, let it go," she breathed under her breath during one of their weekly rounds at Cove Mini Golf. Her mom was performing yet another booty dance to rub in the fact she had knocked Bev's ball into the penultimate windmill and out of bounds with her own. "She is your *shenpa*. Your trigger. Do not succumb to negativity." Of course, that was before the wandering. With Amelia leaving the house unannounced— sometimes with pants, sometimes without; how their roles had reversed—mini golf was no longer on the menu. Her mother was now afraid of random things, like the shower- head, and merely getting her clean was an effort that called for an entire afternoon. Beverly would fill the bathtub and they'd climb in together, like two girls, Bev washing Amelia's back while singing PJ Harvey songs. Despite her flaws, how demeaning and dismissive she had been, Amelia was the one person who loved Beverly, who would probably ever love her, and she felt that love being taken from her neurotransmitter by neurotransmitter. Thanks, universe. Namaste.

At that, Rex Hasselbach threw back his head and released an intimidating bellow of a laugh. "Yeah," he said, wiping his eyes, "namaste." Then he said, Look, I get it, your mom sucks. Do you want to know how I wound up at Jabber- wocky? Beverly nodded. My dad beats the shit out of me, Rex replied. The worst time was while they were watching the third installment in the *Alien* franchise. Rex had an enormous boner for eighties Sigourney Weaver—she was a total babe— and as they reached the climax of the film, where the tiny alien bursts out of Ripley's chest just as she sacrifices herself for her comrades by falling into lava, Rex's dad started making fun of the scene, about how stupid and predictable it was, et cetera. Infuriated by this rude interruption, Rex told his father to shut his bitch mouth. His dad dragged Rex outside, though Rex didn't want to fight and mostly covered his head with his arms. And his dad hit so hard, elbows and fists, that Rex had to go to the hospital for a punctured lung and fractured ribs, where he lied and said he had injured himself by accidentally running into a tree while throwing the football around with his brothers. It was in that hour of darkness that he decided to ruin his father's life. In his dad's name and likeness, Rex set up a variety of fake accounts and started posting the foulest content he could imagine. Racist tirades, rape and death threats, and links to kiddie porn. When his dad lost his job and was arrested, Rex's mother begged Jabberwocky to take him, partly for his protection.

"Isn't this where Ted Kennedy killed that woman?" Clayton asked.

"Mary Jo Kopechne, yes," said Laird. "He was drunk and drove his car off a bridge into a tidal channel."

"What an idiot," Clayton replied. "Can we get lobster rolls after this?"

"We have to find Rex first, Clay," said Beverly. "If we don't find him in a few hours, we're going to have to notify his parents and the police. It will be a total nightmare."

They had crossed over into Chappaquiddick and driven past the beach shacks on their way to the Storrow mansion. It was that part of the island where people said things like,

"We're the third house on the left, the one with the Georgian columns offset in a copse of pines."

"I think this might be a red herring," said Clayton.

"What do you mean?" asked Bev.

"I mean we've been sent on some wild troll goose chase, and it's unlikely he would have made it out this far. It's a red herring."

"We're not characters in a detective novel," said Laird. "It's not like we're running around searching everywhere for a murderer, when, whoops!, turns out it was the butler."

The days were increasingly wistful, and there wasn't much time remaining at camp. Rex might have run away because he was dreading the prospect of confronting his father. If he never went home, he would never have to face him. Similarly, if Beverly left her mother in that home, she wouldn't have to reckon with their dynamic. She was wracked with panic that Rex was desperate enough to do something so rash that going home would no longer be an option. Beverly had to find him.

"What do we do?" Laird asked, ringing the doorbell one more time as they stood shuffling their feet on the Storrow porch. "Nobody's here."

"Maybe they're out back," Beverly said.

Out back, the Storrow pool was empty. Potato chips and floats in the shape of orca whales littered the concrete. Only three elderly gents in a hot tub remained, with identical gray hair and leathery man breasts visible above the burbling waterline. The last guests had made their goodbyes about an hour ago. Though one of them seemed to remember that a groomsman in the wedding of Jenny Barnes had mentioned picking up his new pal Rex—or maybe it was his new pal Bax. Jenny was getting married that afternoon in a tent near the Gay Head Lighthouse. Rex Hasselbach might have decided to go along and gate-crash.

"I told you it was a red herring," Clayton muttered as they walked back to the car.

Clayton Wheeler stuffed his mouth with some more of those puff pastry things and grabbed a couple cups of shrimp ceviche off the tray of a cater waiter. So far, crashing the Barnes wedding reception was the best idea the group had come up with all day. He could hang back and watch the shenanigans while Bev and Lare Bear did the dirty work. "No way is blood thicker than water," he said to himself. Everything in life was made from water, including blood. In order to exist, blood needed water. Not fifteen minutes back, the bride had gotten into a hissy spat with her mother and stomped off in lacy flounces—it was kind of like watching an ice-cream sundae get pissed off—to the bland arms of her new husband. How many of these people hated each other but had shown up out of obligation? Romantic love was a more authentic form of love because you had to consciously choose your life companion. Clayton could safely say that he cared for Nadejda, the

Bulgarian girlfriend he had met while on a two-week archaeology trip during his spring semester—Bulgaria apparently
had untold Thracian treasures—more than his siblings. After
spending a whole day wheeling away excess dirt while the experts brushed at some poor dead guy's thousand-year-old eye
sockets, he and his new besties had visited a bar where they
hadn't been carded. Clay looked up from his foamy beer, beheld a mane of platinum locks, and was immediately smitten.

One night, as they cuddled after Clayton had finished rubbing his cock between Nadejda's breasts, he told her about the
article. A friend of his mom's had emailed his mom, and his
mom had forwarded to him, an article about the discovery in
Laos of cave art that depicted an infant abandoned in the wilderness and subsequently adopted by the tribe who rescued
it. "Families like yours go back to the beginning of time," his
mom's friend had written. The article went on to say that the
ancient Greeks and Romans also practiced adoption. Em-
peror Augustus himself had been an adopted child. Nadejda
responded by kissing Clayton on the cheek and murmuring,
"That is beautiful," but Clayton thought her reaction was fat-
uous. It was the first time he had felt his erection, and his
affection, wilt a little in her presence. When Clayton told Rex
about the article, however, Rex had shrugged and said, "If you
ask me, adoption is pretty nice. Why do you feel unwanted?
You were intentionally selected out of thousands. They could
have picked someone else, but they chose you. Sometimes
your real family doesn't have to give you up to not want you.

My brothers and my dad constantly let me know what a piece of trash I am, so maybe you should start counting your blessings." At first Clayton thought that was the remark of a tool, but after a while Rex's insight was kind of comforting. His adopted parents could have asked for another, but they went with him. And he was their first baby, before the addition of Eleanora from Niger or Gil from Ecuador.

Clay sought out the lobster bisque shooters and crunchy spring rolls favored by the bridesmaids. Maybe the problem was that nowadays the world was filled with too many god-forsaken people. When we were living in nomadic tribal hut societies like the cave art guys in Laos, everybody knew everybody else by name. That meant if you were sick or needed extra boar meat that month, your tribesmen would chip in to help a buddy out, but if you were a dickhead, they'd bang a gong and gather around and stone you to death. It was intimate. Corporate jack-offs couldn't waltz in, swindle you out of hearth and hut, then not have to look you in the eye. Trolls couldn't Photoshop a hot dog in your mouth with impunity or tweet that you were a dead ringer for Rob Reiner from *All in the Family* and keep mentioning you in their threads about Rob Reiner from *All in the Family*. You belonged somewhere. On the flip side, you were also stuck with those people. In the modern world, you might be easily forgotten, but you could also carve out your own niche. You could find where you belonged. His interest in archaeology stemmed from that very reason. Outside of Varna, assisting in hauling up femurs and copper needles from the earth, he knew as much history of these long dead as he did his biological parents. There was something elegant, familiar even, about an anonymous set of bones. He guessed that was ultimately why he tagged along to go get Rex. "Thanks, man," was what Clayton owed to Rex. "You helped me keep things in perspective," he would say nonsarcastically, then add, "And your dad and brothers are jerks. Don't let anyone tell you that you're trash. No way is blood thicker than water."

"Have you seen Laird?" Beverly asked, sidling up to him and grabbing a glass of champagne in the process.

"I thought he was with you."

"He was, but then I started asking the best man about Rex, and when I turned around, he was gone."

"I'm not looking for *both* him and Rex," Clayton replied. "We should have agreed on a place to meet in case we got separated, like at an amusement park. If nothing else, see you in front of the Tower of Terror at four o'clock."

"It's not as though it matters," said Bev. "The wedding party didn't have the foggiest clue about Rex. He isn't here."

"Maybe he is here," Clay replied. "Maybe he hit it off with the maid of honor and is getting lucky behind some bushes."

"Rex isn't like that," quoth Bev.

"He's a teenage male," Clayton said. "He's like that. Maybe he's fucking your mom."

"Go to hell." Beverly shotgunned a second glass of champagne. Holy balls, she sure was touchy today.

"By the way, you and Lare gonna make it official?"

"Oh please," said Bev. "There isn't a woman left in the universe who can get Laird's broken Bunsen burner fired up again."

"Want to wait for him at the car and smoke?"

"Yeah, I say we bail before the insincere toasts."

Bread-crumbing tobacco as they walked away from the white wedding tent down the hill to the parking lot, Clayton rolled them a sloppy J. They arrived pleasantly stoned to Bev's Volkswagen, where Laird was slumped in the driver's seat, his public television science expert forehead resting forlornly on the steering wheel. He had not, as Clayton hypothesized, had a myocardial infarction, but rather was asleep, roasting in the sun.

Laird Hunt guffawed to himself that if you ever came to doubt the outcome of the Stanford Prison Experiment, the sadistic behavior of test subjects when given power over others, you'd only have to look at the immediate family of the man marrying Jenny Barnes. Talk about bona fide dyed-in-the-wool pricks. They were probably still gloating among themselves for taking massive multimillion-dollar bonuses during the subprime mortgage crisis. There was something especially grotesque in the backward tilt of their heads as they slurped oysters from the raw bar. It made Laird's stomach turn. He hadn't undertaken this journey of self-discovery in order to spy on smug rich people enjoying aphrodisiacs. The Jabs were the scions of the one percent, but they were the kids these blowhards were ashamed of, the dirty little secrets they didn't want their investment cohorts to know about, so Laird didn't mind them. But he sure as hell wasn't going to suffer through the simpering celebrations of run-of-the-mill one percenters. The next time he caught someone posing for another cheesy smartphone picture, he'd venture on a stroll toward the lighthouse. Couldn't a single soul, besides the hired photographer, capture the moment with a regular camera? It wasn't as if weddings served as anything other than a distraction from entropy, from the fact that we're screwed. Do you like sticking it in your attractive wife? Do you like your sprinkler system? Do you like having a working pancreas? Too bad, because all that can change faster than you can say "Book of Job."

That was it. A crowd was tapping on their screens to memorialize inebriated fraternity chums in disheveled suits humping the bride. Flinging his way past the plastic flaps into the stinging bright outdoors, he reflected there was something oddly peaceful about an island. A feeling suffused through one's whole body of having fled from the world. It was like being mentally cradled. Was he ready to go home? The paperwork had been filed, but both his ex-wife, Sherri, and his son emphasized in their communiqués that he was welcome to move back whenever he wanted. But he hadn't fully analyzed the impulse that had prompted him to jump ship and dogpaddle toward the genteel harbor of Martha's Vineyard in the first place. The one thing he knew was that the Fetal Pig Incident had something to do with it. He had blithely been going about business as usual, ordering the little oinkers preserved in gelatin for that year's batch of sophomores wrapping up their anatomy unit. After twenty years of teaching, he had become an expert in the signs that a teen was anorexic or self-harming or into drugs. Hence, it was a shock both viscerally and intellectually when Everett Johnson burst in on dissection day with a handgun. "Everett, you're late," he said. "Grab a coat and gloves." The boy in the dour sweatshirt answered by pointing a Glock between Laird's eyeglass lenses. "Silence, Mr. Hunt."

The presence of the weapon didn't sink in everywhere at once. Oblivious, a lab team in the back kept tagging organs. Stacey Weisman was crying, but she had already been crying when her scalpel made its first incisions into gooey skin. Everett trembled, also on the brink of tears. "Listen, Everett," Laird pleaded, "this isn't you. If you put down the gun, I promise you won't get in trouble." Everett screamed, buried the Glock in the belly of a piglet, and fired three rounds. Months later, Laird would find the spot where a bullet had ricocheted off the steel table and embedded in the wall behind the beakers. He should count himself lucky. Nothing had happened. Instead, he found himself nauseated by his job, his son's stinky room filled with dirty boxer briefs, his wife's series of depressed casseroles. Two thoughts picked at his brain. One, where had Everett gotten the gun? Anywhere, he could have secured a gun with ease from anywhere. Second, Everett Johnson was the only face and name he could distinctly remember of his students in the last ten years. It was too late to save Everett Johnson, who was going to pay dearly for the fetal pig. But Laird could save Rex Hasselbach. If he could save Rex Hasselbach, maybe he could save himself—he could go home. At any rate, here he was, at the lighthouse. The lighthouse was nice and lighthousey. A big old lighthouse. He might as well head back to the car.

"Rise and shine, princess," Clayton said, ruffling Laird's widow's peak.

"I'm aware I look like your average science teacher," Laird replied, "but I also think it behooves me to mention I used to compete in amateur boxing."

"Bring it on!" exclaimed Clayton. "Show me, Laird. Who provokes the provocateurs? Who out-memes the dank memers?"

"Don't tempt me."

"Enough, you guys," Beverly said. "Laird, as you can see, no luck at the reception. We should report it."

"Again, I say we're not approaching this from the right angle," replied Clayton. "We should try to get inside the mind of the murderer, so to speak. If you were Rex, where would you go? Think troll."

"Clayton, there's something I've been meaning to ask,"

Laird said. "Why do you work at Jabberwocky? You really don't seem to give a damn." What Laird wanted to say was, *You know how you can calculate the weight of atomic elements in moles? Your appreciation for what we do can't even be measured in moles of hydrogen.*

"I give a damn about the Jabs," Clayton protested. "If you must know, it's my mom's policy that we have to do some form of community service in the summer as long as we live under my parents' roof. Since they're footing the bill for my tuition, that means I still qualify. She wants us to learn the merits of giving back. Think of what I'm sacrificing to be here. Right now I could be at a swank internship or on a yacht. They've grown on me, though. I like Rex."

"You're a real martyr for the cause." Laird rolled his eyes.

For a minute Laird considered the problem of fate, eternal recursion, and the speed of light. It took eight minutes for light from the sun to reach earth. What if, he wondered, we were always living slightly in the past? Not the far-distant past, but, say, only eight minutes past. The decisions we made—for the Jabberwocky trolls to troll, Rex to run away, for Beverly to commit her mother, Laird to abscond from his wife and son—were predestined, thus removing any amount of personal culpability, as well as any amount of hope.

"Get in the car, Clay," Beverly said. "Time to return to camp."

"Don't give up, Bev!" Clay replied. "Maybe Rex went somewhere predictable, where normal people go in their normal lives—to the movies, I know he likes movies, or the beach. We should scope out those spots."

"Where would you suggest we begin? This island is nothing but beachfront property."

"Gay Head Beach is right here. We should pay a visit to Gay Head."

Laird heaved himself out of the Volkswagen. He rubbed his sore sciatic nerve and ambled toward the path leading to the water. "What's up, Lare Lare?" Clayton queried. "Where are you headed, Laird?" Beverly asked. "I'm doing what the kid recommends," Laird replied. Bev and Clay jogged to catch up. "We're coming, too! Wait a sec!" they called. Clay wasn't wrong. It was feasible that Rex wanted to sit by the Atlantic, to be reminded he was alone.

Beverly Greene tugged desiccated crab shells out of the sand and finally realized that the best part of being a free spirit wasn't the artsy companions, drug use, or casual-sex-as-league-sporting-activity, but rather not needing to have a plan. She had been good at that part. She would never have any children. Nor did she have career milestones to brag about, taking into account she didn't have a career in the first place. On the flip side, she would never give birth to a tiny person she'd be forced to watch awaken into consciousness just to start a revenge porn club, like Ethan Fuller, or convince a girl to kill herself, like Michelle Gallant. She also didn't have regrets over failing to learn Italian or travel to Zanzibar or open a fusion restaurant. Perhaps life was better lived in consuming what pleasures were readily available, as opposed to pursuing a given outcome with resolve and passion. However, the part about being a free spirit she hadn't been good at was the letting go part. Her mother was going to die frightened in a room identical to every other room in the Memory Care Ward of the Sundown Institute. Was Beverly supposed to take deep breaths, chant "om" as if nothing were the matter, and reach acceptance of that fact? Well, acceptance could screw itself. She hated acceptance. Looking out over the ocean, she thought, At least the waves will always be mine.

She had hopped on a Greyhound bus to California when she was seventeen, trying not to get up and pee until the designated rest stops. As a result, she had been cut off financially, but it was liberating. Starting out, she worked in a hippie bookstore peddling incense and healing energy crystals to soccer moms and sad widowers. Then she moved into a house share in the Hollywood Hills with some guitarists and sold hot tubs to the stars. They were former B-list actors who still bore atavistic traits from their days on the small screen. Smiling at her with snowy veneers and radioactive tans, they asked several questions about the advantages of wooden versus acrylic models. Those rich old men having a soak in the family five-seater that afternoon in Chappy weren't that different.

The hot tub job was a way to get back on her board. Her room-mates, all of whom she slept with, taught her the basics. Once she learned how to stand up and stopped swallowing salt water, she discovered she loved to surf. Amelia never had to try it herself. Beverly could yet renege on the nursing home. Her decision wasn't irrevocable. To give herself the opportunity to renege but also keep her mind occupied, she had signed up to work at Jabberwocky. Also, she was used to dead-end jobs. But god, she didn't want to offer herself up to the altar of her mother's malice. It didn't matter if the cruelty was now unintentional. As it turned out, it might be a blessing that everything ended. We can love without believing in our capacity to love.

Far off, dolphins curved out of the ocean like gleaming parentheses. How wonderful it would feel to be riding with them, to commune with that sleekness. "There are dolphins living in the Black Sea," Clayton offered. "Plus, they have dolphin shows in the Varna Dolphinarium. It's like the Bulgarian SeaWorld." Laird lightly punched him in the arm. "You do know a lot about Bulgaria. Are you sure you haven't hacked our election?" he asked. "That was Russia," Clayton replied. "Aren't you from there?" Laird winked at Bev. "Nice one, Laird. Excellent trolling. Very funny," Clayton huffed. "Ha ha, everyone, I'm adopted!" On the subject of trolling, Beverly wondered again who had sent those notes to Rex. When she asked Rex who he thought it was, he said, "My dad. I'll bet my brothers are making the drawings, since they liked to tease me about the birthmark, and he's doing the rest. He wants me to know this isn't over." Beverly was skeptical—there wasn't any postage on them! Someone in camp, surely, was the culprit. "It doesn't matter," Rex said. "I can't control him. I can only control myself. And I refuse to spend any more time enabling him to get the better of me." Rex was too wise—he should be the one putting them through trust-building exercises. You can't fix the Amelias of this world. You can only fix yourself. And Beverly wasn't going to wallow in guilt or regret anymore. As if she manifested Rex with that thought, she spotted him. There was no mistaking those towering shoulders or that wine-dark poop emoji. Rex Hasselbach, in rubber ducky swim trunks, snorkel gear on his forehead, was walking along the tide, searching for seashells.

"That's him," Beverly whispered. "Rex Hasselbach. I'm not crazy, right?" Clay and Laird turned their heads in unison to where she pointed, then jumped to their feet.

"Rex! Rex! Over here!" they called. "We're over here, Rex!"

Startled, Rex darted his head around until he recognized them. He gave a small screech. "No!" he cried. "Not yet! I'm not ready to go back!"

He dove in the water, swimming as fast as his arms and legs would take him into the hazy distance. Beverly, Laird, and Clayton ran to the shore and stopped. All three of them were clothed—no one had a suit—and they began sizing up which one was either going to strip butt-naked or plunge in fully dressed to follow after Rex.

"Maybe we should get a lifeguard," Laird suggested.

"Man, he's really booking it," Clayton said.

"Wow," Beverly replied. "Look at him go."

to save the universe,
we must also save ourselves

We are the fans of *Starship Uprising*, and we have gathered together, under the gentle supervision of our godly moderators, to share our love of the hit television show and occasionally rant about politics. Hunkering behind screens, we like and we dislike. Laptops toasty on top of our tummies, we comment. We throw down. We emoji. It's difficult to surmise our actual number—we may be thousands strong, or we may be one insomniac hacker. These episodes got us through rehab when we craved the sweet relief of fermentation, the self-loathing when we were laid off, the despair of existing alone in this world when our mothers died. Nevertheless, there is a caste system to us outcasts. Prove yourself fluent in Kil'aathi, which is a fully realized language with its own grammar and lexicon, and you shall be deemed worthy of our respect and admiration. Assert that your favorite character is Spambot, the accident-prone bartender android who constantly tries to up-sell in the awkwardest of moments and offers unsolicited advice to customers, and you shall be deemed a loser, subject to our derision and relentless mockery. Questions plague us late at night, questions we need answered, such as: If the telepad works by ripping you apart atom by atom and reassembling you in another location, does that mean it is a clone machine? If the replimat converts waste to sustenance, does that mean you're eating shit? If the empath senses the emotions of the crew, does that mean she knows when you are masturbating? At least there is something we unanimously agree on, that Commander Dinara Gorun, played by Faith Massey, embodies the feminine ideal. Tough yet vulnerable, gorgeous but proudly bearing the scars of battle, she was our first crush. We wanted to bed her, or be her, or both. She made us who we are.

This infatuation can be traced back, for a majority of us, to the finale of season one, entitled "Our Nebulous Past." The *Audacity*, a cunning rig of down-on-their-luck interstellar smugglers, was on the run from the Voydals, a ruthless species that enslaved or annihilated every life-form it encountered in its mission to conquer the universe. With the enemy closing in on their hypertrail and their vessel severely damaged, the captain had the *Audacity* steered into a nearby nebula. But this was no ordinary cosmic phenomenon: this nebula was sentient, and once it had other beings to keep it company, it didn't want to let them go. Hallucinations of the dear and departed started to torment everyone on board. So powerful were the hallucinations, so seemingly alive, that those most affected obeyed their hallucinations. They shut off the engines and sabotaged the navigation system. Any who objected were locked inside photon prisons. Only Commander Dinara Gorun, the fearless and straight-talking second-in-command, had the will to resist. She broke out of her photon prison, incapacitated her captors, and restored basic functionality to the *Audacity*. As the starship moved out of the nebula, she lay down in the arms of her mother, who stroked her daughter's hair and sang a lullaby. Dinara hadn't been immune to the hallucinations, but she didn't give in to their siren allure. Even though she had lost more than anyone, her whole family murdered in Voydal internment camps, she was still the baddest bitch in the galaxy.

Sadly, the actress Faith Massey has fallen far short herself of the feminine ideal in the intervening years. At the supermarket, we heave our groceries onto the conveyor belt and glance at the tabloids that document her fluctuating waistline. There she is on a Maui beach in a bikini, bending to pick up a shell, and in case some of us miss it or don't see the problem, the magazine highlights her midsection with a red circle. For a spell, she was also a spokesperson for Skinny Friend, the weight-loss company that produces frozen dinners, which definitely aren't in our shopping carts. What a change from her heyday, when we stared longingly in our living rooms at her figure in that thong leotard and leg warmers emblazoned on

VHS tapes of her workout regimen, *Commander Dinara Gorun's THE BODY*. When she's spotted leaving a doctor's office with an unrecognizable face—her lips puffy and ridiculous as a pool float, her forehead lifted a tad too far, like someone tried to stretch a queen-sized fitted sheet over a king-sized mattress—we judge hard. Commander Dinara Gorun despised falseness, and the sole knife she would be caught dead under is the blade of a sworn foe. We look up the plastic surgeon, and he's so pretty it's almost uncanny. On image search, the waiting area of his practice is suffused with a rosy glow, that come-hither boudoir lighting, and decorated with plush pink fainting sofas. It is labia-chic, what we suppose the inside of a vagina would look like if a vagina were a doctor's office. There is also a noticeable swan theme—swan sculptures, a swan in brush pen for the logo, swan paintings on the walls, including an oil reproduction of a swan winding its bird neck up a woman's thigh.

"The swan," claims the copy on his website, "is the perfect symbol for the process of metamorphosis. The proverbial ugly duckling grows up to be a swan. A swan is ungainly on land, a lumbering beast, but becomes the picture of supreme elegance on water, as stated in the immortal 1956 movie *The Swan*, starring Grace Kelly and Alec Guinness. Helen of Troy, the most breathtaking woman to ever be born, according to myth, was hatched from a swan egg after Zeus, in the form of a swan, seduced Leda." We compose scathing, one-star reviews on his business page. "Faith Massey would look better if she were hit by a bus," we opine. "Faith has been infested by the Dolospores," we hypothesize, "the outer space parasite that kills you by burrowing through your nose into your brain and then reanimating your corpse until you decay." We think she should sue. "You are a quack, a charlatan," the more sophisticated among us accuse. "Swan fucker," the less-than-sophisticated insult, before the reviews are removed. We mourn the end of our childhoods. "Thanks for ruining our childhoods," we write. On social media, Faith Massey condemns our behavior, but that doesn't bother us. "Commander Dinara Gorun," she scolds, "defended the oppressed against the powerful. She would never hide in the shadows, flinging hateful slurs." A photo of Commander Dinara Gorun posed arms-on-hips in a heroine stance accompanies the post. "Cunt," we reply. "Thanks for ruining our childhoods."

Anyway, we still binge-watch (or rather, binge-rewatch) the show. We continue to collect the *Starship Uprising* memorabilia, the uniforms of the crew or regalia of the various aliens; the mugs, the three-ring binders, the lunch boxes with their incredibly shiny cartoon boobs; the prosthetic silicone forehead of concentric crop circles that was worn by Faith Massey herself and we purchased at a bargain (in terms of what it's really worth) on an auction site; the Commander Dinara Gorun action figurines and dolls, some of them adult dolls that are anatomically accurate, which we like very much. Our enthusiasm for the conventions is also steady. Donning our costumes, we are a rambunctious horde of spandex and leather, a crushing throng of selfie sticks that poke each other in the back. When the day is over, we descend upon the nearby overpriced bistros and trendy bars, where we order artisanal cocktails in character. But until we hit the town, we wait in line to meet Faith, to have her autograph her headshot for forty dollars or an item of the aforementioned memorabilia. If we're one of the kookier types, we might present a sonogram of our unborn baby and proclaim, "We're naming her Dinara!" To which Faith might blink a lot and mutter, touched, we're sure, "I'm honored." She's smaller in person, and that brings out our protective side. Before parting, we clasp her hand between our sweaty palms and we demonstrate our appreciation with a sincere, "Thank you." In heartfelt tones, we say, "Thank you for our childhoods."

Often, we joke that the pageantry of the conventions is like that episode of *Starship Uprising* entitled, simply, "Surfaces." In it, the *Audacity* is visiting Concupiscens after the successful delivery of a weapons cache into territory dominated by the Voydals. Concupiscens is a pleasure planet renowned not only for its flora and fauna, but also the orgies hosted by the Scensates, its native humanoids. Despite the paradise that surrounds her, Commander Dinara Gorun is unable to relax and participate in the sexcapades. A hunky waiter delivers gourmet replimat rations to her capsule quarters and strips, assuming she wants to mate, and she stops him to ask, "Where are the old people?" Turns out, the society of the Scensates is a hierarchy founded on beauty. Those who are most attractive get to procreate in the orgy pits and lead the government. Those who are least attractive, including the elderly—for what is more hideous than mortality?—are forbidden from producing offspring and forced to work far beneath the surface of the planet, to become invisible. Strangely, the rest of the crew isn't that disturbed by the notion of banishing a homely faction of your population to be slaves. Everyone shrugs and admits they had a fun time. Are we any better than the Scensates? True, not that many of us could be considered particularly beautiful, but we parade around in our outfits with an air of superiority and rip on ensembles worse than ours. We vow to be better fans.

Surprisingly, though perhaps it should not be so surprising, there are some among us who do not wish to be better fans. They are the truly lost, those who delight in hate and embrace chaos. Beneath the troll bridge of their IP addresses, they grind their axes and fashion their memes. As their mascot, they have adopted Chokut Sar, leading general of the Voydals and a gleeful advocate of torture. He laughs at us from the tiny rectangle of their profile pictures, if it were possible for him to laugh. In contrast to the Kil'aathi such as Commander Dinara Gorun, a bunch of purple, peaceful hippies forced into war against their nature, the Voydals look like insects, with mantis legs and bulging glossy eyes. Hive-minded, they communicate telepathically from antennae notched with thorns that are also used as weapons and thus they have no mouths. What they have in place of a mouth resembles an anus. The mouth-anus sort of clenches and releases when they project their thoughts into another's thoughts. It is supposed to be intimidating, but we consider their proboscises about as scary as a bouquet of flaccid penises. These groupies of evil post screencaps of Chokut Sar interrogating rebels, his antennae fastened to their temples. "I will break you," Chokut Sar promises. Or he's covered in blood, having paid a visit to the internment camps, and declaring, "The lesser races are meant to serve." Gangs of these angry young men (they are always angry young men) in their pathetic masks of extraterrestrial bullies purposely bump into us at events and harass us in the bathroom. Meanwhile, they chant the mantra of the Voydals: "We are gods. Obey or die."

Pasty as the bottom-feeders that feast on outer space trash, with genitals as unused as those of the Celebos, geniuses that went extinct from the galaxy because they regarded bumping uglies as icky—that is how we imagine these Voydal worshippers. It's easy enough to block their accounts until one of us, a fan famous in his own domain, a gamer called Gangrene-Pete, unwittingly instigates a controversy that makes them impossible to ignore. GangrenePete is the creator of a video channel with millions of subscribers where he documents himself playing through vintage console favorites such as *Castlevania: Symphony of the Night* or, more recently, *Starship Uprising: The Voydal Apocalypse*. At some point, GangrenePete was asked why he decided on the name GangrenePete, and he said he decided on the name GangrenePete because he is "raw and disgusting." For several hours (curated into a playlist of fifteen-minute installments), GangrenePete controlled the tiny, pixelated avatar of Commander Dinara Gorun and gleefully slaughtered Voydals with her ray gun, simultaneously noting what a fox the actress Faith Massey had been and how he had spent his adolescence beating his Pete meat to a poster of her or the covers on the VHS tapes of her workout regimen, *Commander Dinara Gorun's THE BODY*. Whenever she died, forcing him to restart the level, he would shout, "That Voydal is raping her!" In response, the hostess of a feminist web series entitled *Nerd Girls Resist!* proceeded to shame GangrenePete for essentially being an insensitive asshole who normalized sexual assault.

Immediately the Voydal army leapt to the defense of GangrenePete and argued that the overreaction by *Nerd Girls Resist!* to GangrenePete minimized the experiences of those who had actually been sexually assaulted and that maybe she'd stop with the self-righteous attitude if she were properly boned. *Nerd Girls Resist!* struck back with a long montage of female characters being brutalized in games, interspersed with statistics on violence against women. Then a conservative media pundit picked up the story for his "Kids These Days" segment and said that no one cared about Faith Massey, as she was a washed-up actress from the era of the dial-up modem who had put on a not-insignificant amount of weight and that this "uppity" web series hostess should shut up and determine "better things to do with that mouth." Horrified as well as amused, we were inseparable from our electronics while we proposed a myriad of ideas, both serious and absurd, for what anything with a mouth could do with that mouth, such as sticking multiple Peeps marshmallows inside, or a big shark mouth noshing on a baby seal, et cetera. One of us went as far as to share a gif of a Voydal mouth doing its sphincteresque dance along with the question, "What if you don't have a mouth?" Reluctantly, we were obligated to remind everyone to "Check your mouth privilege."

Some of us also felt obligated during this GangrenePete fiasco to remind the others that not all the fans of *Starship Uprising* were straight white men, as evinced by *Nerd Girls Resist!* We hailed from every demographic, and we adored Faith Massey because, in her, we got to see ourselves on television. Yes, Commander Dinara Gorun was stunningly attractive, but her looks weren't her defining characteristic. She was tough yet vulnerable, purple and weird and still out-of-this-world sexy; she didn't fit into any established mold. So whenever Faith Massey was reduced to a body (or, simply, the VHS tapes of *THE BODY*), it made it seem like Commander Dinara Gorun—and, therefore, we—never really mattered, as though women should just be tossed out of the air lock when their twenties are over. And we knew there were those among us who griped that they would have been involuntary Celebos or in the Concupiscens slave caste but who nonetheless picked apart Faith's appearance. Who cared about her plastic surgery or her weight or her tits? We thought we were here to celebrate a thing we loved that somehow, miraculously, got made. Shut up, we were told, everyone has moved on. We were so whiny, possibly menstruating. But those directly involved would not move on, not GangrenePete, who continued to avow that he was a good guy beneath the rotting persona, not the hostess of *Nerd Girls Resist!*, who had been accumulating death threats from Voydals, and especially not Faith Massey.

Faith Massey was invited to be a guest on the talk show *The Alcove*, where she was interviewed by Cindy Withers, previously a prominent reporter but currently on *The Alcove*. "How are you holding up?" Cindy asked, then nodded profusely as Faith replied, "Honestly? It's been difficult." In her gray cashmere sweater that she hugged comfortingly around herself, with sleepless gray circles around her gray eyes, Faith came clean about her struggle with addiction and clinical depression. She was healthy and sober—here she raised a wrist ringed by a bracelet that chimed with recovery coins—but the GangrenePete thing had brought back some extremely painful memories. It was common internet lore that on the set of *Starship Uprising* she had a brief romance with Jake Knight, her costar who went on to have a fruitful career in car insurance commercials. (Though when we got wise to that piece of trivia, we were a bit obsessed and created our own fan art depicting what they looked like in flagrante delicto, supernovae blazing in the background.) When it ended, she was devastated that she had to continue to be entangled romantically with the cocksure yet tender captain of the *Audacity* on-screen when they were no longer entangled off-screen. As she waited in wardrobe, preparing herself to film a kiss, she started crying and explained the story to the man applying her forehead. What happened next she had discussed ad nauseam: how she and the makeup artist fell in love, had a wedding with a cake shaped as a starship, conceived a daughter. But what she had been too scared to discuss was how he became a jealous husband, how he hit her and gave her bruises, and how, as she sat before him in the prep chair, he covered up the purple that he had made with more purple.

"He threw our dog off the deck," Faith confessed, impressionistic with tears. "He threw your dog off the deck?" Cindy Withers asked unnecessarily, a rhetorical tactic she frequently deployed throughout her stint on *The Alcove*. Yes, Faith said. He threw our dog off the deck. After the finale of season seven, when Commander Dinara Gorun is taken hostage by the Voydals and is tortured telepathically for her refusal to cooperate in tracking down the *Audacity*, they hosted a wrap party at their house in the Hollywood Hills. Her husband saw her chatting with—guess who—Jake Knight and accused her of cheating. She denied it, but it's possible she was slightly tipsy and it's also possible that she was flirting a little. As punishment, he threw the dog off the deck. The pooch fractured a paw, the canine metacarpal bones. Post-fracture, the dog had this goofy gait; families at the park would kindly inquire as to whether she had rescued the dog from an abusive situation, and she was tempted to inform them that she was the abusive situation. "You were not the abusive situation," Cindy Withers nasally consoled. "No, I was the abusive situation," Faith disagreed. Throwing the dog off the deck was not the last straw. Divorce wasn't on the table until the show was canceled. During the interim, her daughter was forced to see her mother hurt over and over, and then, when the physical abuse was over, she was forced to see her mother abuse herself with booze, then with prescription painkillers and assorted muscle relaxants. Faith Massey was not a good mother.

"My daughter cut me out of her life," Faith lamented. Her ex deviously and sociopathically turned their daughter against Faith. He had lied and said that Faith had been having an affair with Jake Knight for their entire marriage, that she had screamed at him how she wished their daughter had been her daughter with Jake Knight. "I want her to know"— Faith choked out the words, staring directly at us—"Ashley, if you watch this, I miss you so much and I'm sorry I wasn't there when you needed me." She reminisced about their first holiday together after the divorce, that Halloween her daughter had requested to dress up as Commander Dinara Gorun. It wasn't cool to go as Commander Dinara Gorun anymore, but Faith dug out her forehead and her dusty ray gun from storage. (Now we absolutely do not regret paying so much on an auction site for the bona fide silicone prosthetic forehead worn by Faith Massey in *Starship Uprising*.) Here, savvy editors at *The Alcove* displayed a faded and crinkled photo of Faith standing beside the girl Commander Dinara Gorun, one of those photos from a disposable camera once conveniently printed in the pharmacy next to tubes of hemorrhoid cream. "Isn't she cute?" Faith was syrupy and melodious, the voice of nostalgia—a feeling to which we were not unaccustomed. "That is the best compliment I've ever received, her trick-or-treating as me." We're not too proud to admit that we shed a tear ourselves when she described smearing purple powder across her daughter's cheeks and lowering onto her precious upturned face the silicone forehead as though it were a sacred crown. As Faith did her daughter's makeup, she was overwhelmed with love.

We are overwhelmed with love for Faith Massey. It is interesting how her story compares to the plot of the episode she mentioned on *The Alcove* that inadvertently caused her dog to get thrown off the deck, the finale of season seven, entitled "The Secrets We Keep." When Commander Dinara Gorun is telepathically tortured by the Voydals, Chokut Sar himself conducts the interrogation. The *Audacity* is en route to the headquarters of their empire to rescue her, despite the risks. Besides, the safest place to hide is often in plain sight. In between mind probes, Commander Dinara Gorun bonds with her fellow prisoners. They, too, are hiding in plain sight. The Voydals can't torture them for information if they don't know anything, so the rebels have figured out a method to embed critical communications into tumors that are grown inside the bodies of those who volunteer to be runners. Lucky runners who reach their intended destinations will have their tumors painlessly harvested and decrypted. Unlucky runners must make peace with destiny, that either the Voydals or the tumors will kill them—whichever comes first. Their sacrifice has been worth it, as the Voydals have been unable to crack the cancerous code. But the cruel twist is this: After the *Audacity* arrives, Commander Dinara Gorun refuses to leave with her crew. Chokut Sar possesses some of her memories, and she some of his. Torture acts like a narcotic for both torturer and victim, and it is highly addictive. Such violence can wipe out your body as well as your spirit, is the lesson we learn, like it did to Faith Massey. What's amazing is how *Starship Uprising* has stayed topical and relevant to this day, so ahead of its time.

Our faith in Faith Massey has been betrayed with yet another very public fracas—and we tried so hard to get over ourselves, our distaste for her atrocious plastic surgery and her disappointing career after the run of *Starship Uprising*. There was supposed to be a spin-off focused on Commander Dinara Gorun! There was supposed to be a dark and edgy Oscar-bait movie where we could ogle her tits! Instead, there were occasional spots on lawyer procedurals, cameos as herself on sitcoms, and, of course, Skinny Friend. After her moving tell-all on *The Alcove*, which garnered considerable clicks and advertising revenue, we reached out to Faith and expressed our sympathy. We risked our dignity and our privacy as we related our own paths through rehab when we craved the sweet relief of fermentation, the self-loathing when we were laid off, the despair of existing alone in this world when our mothers died. Some of the messages we composed using pen and paper, which we then sent in the mail using postage we bought with money! For our online shops, we crafted Commander Dinara Gorun tote bags and pins. Who will buy this unwanted stock? No one is who, not since one of us has courageously come forth, an erstwhile personal assistant who must unfortunately remain anonymous due to strict nondisclosure agreements, to reveal that everything Faith Massey divulged in that interview was a total fabrication. The Voydals gloat as though there is no tomorrow. Their leader, the merciless Chokut Sar, doesn't pretend to be someone he's not—he's a bigoted and genocidal giant bug, that's who he is.

To begin, the personal assistant had to make it clear that Faith Massey was by no means sober. She was still a pill-popping drunkard, though the substance of choice during the assistant's tenure was weed. The assistant wasn't concerned about the weed, not as much as the opioids anyway, so she became the contact for the weed dealer. The weed dealer was friendly, almost overeager to help, which made sense because Faith consumed enough weed weekly to satisfy the needs of a minor campus fraternity. He had the assistant examine a mole on his back, right above the band of his underwear, to see if she thought he "should be worried." His underwear was a pair of Calvin Klein lime-green boxer briefs. So that was a fact the assistant would never be able to forget—she knew the brand of underwear worn by Faith Massey's weed dealer. Secondly, the assistant had held back our beloved celebrity's hair while she vomited an eclectic combo of benzos and tequila, and in between her gagging, Faith let it slip that her daughter probably *was* her daughter with Jake Knight. And Jake, by the way, was quite the douchebag. Both Faith and Jake were invited to be panelists at a futuristic film festival in Miami, where they debated inspiring activism via outer space allegory. When the panel was finished, as they were chauffeured to the hotel in a limo, he hung his torso through a window and shouted at ladies in the street, "I'm Captain John Augustus Flint from *Starship Uprising!* Don't you want to fuck me?" At the hotel, the assistant was relaxing in the sauna when he walked in and urged her to suck his cock. That's why she was fired—full disclosure: Faith was not happy that Jake Knight was more into the assistant than her, even though the assistant didn't want anything to do with his decrepit sci-fi herpes dick.

Lastly, the assistant confirmed that Faith Massey was estranged from her daughter, but the estrangement was one hundred percent Faith's fault. The daughter had been dating a focus puller in Venice Beach who was into "unexpected creampies" and had gotten her pregnant. Faith begged her daughter to have an abortion, but the daughter decided to keep the baby. Then Faith said, "Okay, keep the baby, but break up with the boyfriend. I'll support you." When the daughter refused to break up with the boyfriend, Faith cut the daughter out of her life, and not vice versa. It had nothing to do with the makeup artist ex-husband, who was abusive; that wasn't exaggerated. Speaking of the makeup artist ex-husband, Faith had been so glad to indulge in the narrative of doing her daughter's makeup for Halloween. What she somehow failed to mention was the incident when she was super-wasted—again—and insisted the assistant do her up as Commander Dinara Gorun. They used her ex-husband's makeup kit, which she inexplicably had kept. In a fluffy bathrobe with a towel wound around her hair, Faith looked like a retired Commander Dinara Gorun on a cruise. As Faith caught sight of her purple reflection, she sobbed. She buried her face in the assistant's shirt and left a permanent impression from the expired professional cosmetics, as though the shirt were a Kil'aathi Shroud of Turin. Her ex-husband had enjoyed screwing her after tapings as Commander Dinara Gorun. No one had ever loved her for herself. Pressing his forearm into her windpipe, he demanded that she recite her famous catchphrase, so she moaned, "To save the universe, we must also save ourselves."

Guilt haunts us as we comment, as we like and we dislike, as we throw down, as we emoji. Though we are not as responsible as some for having messed up Faith Massey, we cannot deny that we have not loved her for herself. (Some of us have been attempting for a while to point out that our love is fickle, but when we try to point out that we've been pointing that out, we are told to shut up and that we are probably menstruating.) It's like that episode of *Starship Uprising* that opens with the death of the ship's counselor from a random tele-pad accident, entitled "Mirror, Mirror." Until a new empath can be located, the crew has to make do with a holographic counselor, otherwise known as a Computerized Affective Relating Lifefacsimile, or CARL. How CARL works is that it scans your brain in order to take bits and pieces of those you love—your mother's smile, your dad's dad humor—and project the ultimate composite of a person you're most likely to trust. Then it uses a technique invented by famous twentieth century psychologist Carl Rogers, wherein the CARL merely repeats back to you what you said so it can get you to spill your guts. "I'm feeling sort of disconnected from everything lately," you'll say, and it will repeat, "You're feeling disconnected lately." You'll say, "I'm upset because Portia dumped me," and so it will repeat, "Portia dumped you." Perhaps you'll say, "I don't need therapy. I know what's wrong with me. A genetically engineered virus wiped out our colony on Rentathus Nine. That's what's wrong with me," so it will repeat, "A virus wiped out your colony on Rentathus Nine." The crew stops socializing, instead preferring to spend their recreational allotment with CARL, a portion of them becoming smitten with the holographic counselor. When the replacement empath arrives, she promptly turns off the program.

However, the guilt only lasts a remorseful thread or so before one of us points out that no matter what she is going through, Faith Massey chose to deceive her fans, and we are once more consumed by rage. We say adios to our lingering inhibitions and team up with the Voydals for some seriously off-the-hook trolling. On social media, we manipulate pictures of Commander Dinara Gorun to include block lettering of "Cheater" or "Junkie" or "Terrible Mother" and we tag Faith. To the covers of *Commander Dinara Gorun's THE BODY* we add "of lies" so it reads Commander Dinara Gorun's *THE BODY OF LIES*. To Skinny Friend frozen dinner packaging, we change Skinny Friend to Not So Skinny Friend. The drawing entitled *The Rape of Commander Dinara Gorun* depicting the rape of Commander Dinara Gorun by a Voydal is taking it too far, we agree, but we require catharsis. "Thanks for ruining our childhoods," we write, and we send messages composed using pen and paper, using postage we bought with money! When the tabloids document her stumbling out of a bar and a breast with nipple hanging out of her shirt along with the headline "Faith Massey Meltdown," it is what she deserves. And hey, we finally saw her rack, even if we had to wait decades. Jake Knight issues a statement, in which he pledges his eternal affection for Faith Massey. Also, he does not have herpes, and certain ex-employees might want to be more circumspect about what they blab about on the internet, as someone, such as an attorney, might put two and two together.

An announcement is planned at Comic-Con in San Diego, where there will be a cast reunion for *Starship Uprising*. We speculate as to what it is, but many of us are adamant that we must boycott. That said, we are too curious for our own good and can't stay away. Donning our costumes, we are a rambunctious horde of spandex and leather, a crushing throng of selfie sticks that poke each other in the back, and this time we have brought signs. Our signs are inscribed with NERD GIRLS RESIST! or I HAVE FAITH or I AM CAPTAIN JOHN AUGUSTUS FLINT, DON'T YOU WANT TO FUCK ME? On stage, the crew of the *Audacity* gathers holding hands while the trumpety theme song warbles through the air. When Faith Massey is introduced, there are boos, but she silences us with a finger to her lips and shushing noises. "The story of Commander Dinara Gorun is one of survival," she whispers into the microphone, "of fighting for what's right, the odds be damned. It's a story that's desperately needed by another generation." And then it happens—a Chokut Sar mask sails across the sea of us, and it almost floats (that's how we will recall the altercation later, while we upload our phone video) as it pauses for a second in front of a frightened Faith Massey, like it was deciding if this is really what it wanted to do, before thwapping her in the face with its floppy insect antennae dildos. A brawl breaks out between Voydals and a purple posse of jacked Kil'aathi as she flees the scene, hysterical. Alas, the rest of us do not find out what was in the announcement.

Allegedly, we were to be told there was a completely fresh season of *Starship Uprising* in development to debut on a popular streaming service. Elatedly, we practically soil ourselves with anticipation and pray that our actions have not jeopardized the triumphant return of our favorite show. To our relief, production moves forward, minus Jake Knight because of increasing evidence regarding his sexual harassment, though we assume this will have no lasting ramifications. He is Jake Knight, and how can anything challenge a man like that? And when does Faith Massey not confront a challenge? Faith Massey takes selfies on set as she's done up in the purple skin and silicone concentric crop circle forehead of the Kil'aathi by a man who is not her ex-husband. She also takes a selfie with her daughter and her baby, Joey, and captions it thus: "I have reunited with Ashley. My grandson is a joy. One day, I hope my fans can also share the gift of forgiveness." When the episodes premiere, we build a nest of blankets, memorabilia, and food (with, yes, Skinny Friend frozen dinners) on our couches and settle in for the long haul. In the first episode, Commander Dinara Gorun is thrown back in time and discovers that the woman who rescued her from the Voydal internment camps was herself. With gravitas, we recite to our televisions, "To save the universe, we must also save ourselves." The following episode, the main computer is endowed with sentience and goes crazy, so they provide it with porn from a race of sado-masochistic shape-shifters to chill it out. "Put on the ball gag and turn into a gorilla," a shape-shifter instructs. "Now bark like a dog, as a gorilla." This thrills us, and we hashtag up a storm. Even the Voydals are impressed and pleased. *Starship Uprising* is as wonderful as it ever was. We forgive.

realtor to the damned

Before relatives could ruin our fun with anecdotes, my wife and I made a game of guessing the histories of the dead. There was Greg, who was convinced that when he wore his bifocals with owls on the rims that he could decode messages from outer space in his crossword puzzle. And Beth became bored with knitting scarves, so her many amorphous blobs of yarn were chastity belts for retirees with arthritic hips. Dan was aroused by the sight and smell of cocktail olives, but the effectiveness of old jars wore off eventually, which was why he had so many jars of cocktail olives. Yolanda crafted those paper cranes out of the obituaries she recognized.

What pathos we inflicted upon the deceased's potted plants. Once, we discovered a closet filled with golf balls. Upon their inadvertent release, the golf balls sprang around the foyer like giant popcorn kernels that refused to bloom.

"He was a sportswriter," I said. "He kept a golf ball for every tournament he was assigned to cover for his paper."

"He had that disorder that compels you to eat objects," she replied. "This is his food."

The owner had been a woman who hunted for golf balls while she took long walks to think about God. Her son explained this to us while sobbing, so we kindly inquired whether we should dispose of the golf balls for him, and he whimpered, No, thanks, I'll take them to the range.

"His mom's going to be mad he got rid of those balls by working on his swing," I said after he was out of hearing range at the golf range. "What if that means she can't move on?" I can recommend a reputable moving company, but not one prepared to move the incorporeal.

"Where are my Titleists?" my wife spooky-joked. "Where are they, Gary?"

It was me who ruined our fun by debating the ethics of reaping a profit from haunted properties. Did we have an obligation to list ghosts on the condition assessment?

"Even the dead need a qualified professional," she reasoned.

Her practical wisdom was why I married my wife. Thus, when I was touring a listing to take inventory—black mold, alas, but crown molding, hallelujah—and there was a dachshund in the refrigerator, I immediately texted my wife to get her opinion: *Hey, honey, found a dachshund in the refrigerator*. A ghostly ellipsis surprisingly indicated she indeed had an opinion about this development, and after an eternity, she texted back: *Dick pic?* I complied, from astonishment, and snapped a photo down my pants. But I wasn't expecting a text because, like those whose houses we sold, my wife is also dead.

Now send me the dachshund, she texted.

I sent her the dachshund.

Since I am a professional, I should confess that I have never seen a ghost. The closest I have come to a ghost is a sonogram, which is the opposite of a ghost, the presaging of a life, unless the life is never born. With my wife's miscarriages, my sales slipped until I was ranked last. When you're last, you get what no one wants; in the case of Florida real estate, that was the weird homes of the elderly, recently dear and departed. To pass the time, my wife, herself a trained realtor on leave, read ghost stories aloud, and we had a lot of time to pass in no show showings where a ghost would have been a welcome relief from the drudgery—a good name for an evil spirit, Drudgery. "One should accept ghosts very much as one accepts fire," my wife read from a book by Robert von Ranke Graves, his actual name. "It is not really an element, not a principle of motion, not a living creature—though a house can catch it from its neighbours. It is an event."

Fair enough, Rob, but if ghosts are events, then each instant counts as a ghost. The car accident that killed my wife is a ghost. Rumor has it that there's an astronomer ghost who occupies the derelict telescope at the Ritter Planetarium at the University of Toledo in Ohio. Celestial light is what's left of stars long extinguished, so the stargazer ghost is a ghost observing ghosts. And when a comet cuts its wake through the black, it's called an apparition. Science, too, it seems, supports the notion that everything is ghostly.

If you are my wife, I texted, *what advice did you give to women who were desperate to become pregnant?*

When I first got pregnant, she texted back, *I thought I was turning into a werewolf.*

Do you think werewolves get premenstrual syndrome but for becoming a werewolf in addition to regular premenstrual syndrome?

I think female werewolves go into heat. They don't have periods. So they don't experience premenstrual syndrome. But the general werewolf population gets premenstrual syndrome for changing into a werewolf and that's why werewolves are a matriarchal society.

Maybe you are my wife.

You are not my husband.

The deceased with a grand piano in perfect tune and without a trace of dust was easy—concert pianist, I concluded. But he didn't fulfill his dream of playing Carnegie Hall, therefore he returns as a ghost night after night to practice his Rachmaninoff. I was so lazy, unlike that pianist ghost I invented. My wife could be a harsh ghost critic. Where was my imagination? Clearly, this owner had been devoured by the piano.

Look at it, she insisted, doesn't it look hungry? Speaking of imagination, I said, you always go for the meals!

Tinkly piano music kept coming from a place that was and wasn't the piano. My wife and I started to fear the piano truly was possessed, but then the niece of the deceased informed us that there was a school for gifted children down the street. Sometimes we forgot there were children in Sarasota County, despite trying to have our own. We strolled to the school for gifted children, and outside there were boys fishing in a construction hole, though we didn't know if they were gifted boys. Gators sunned themselves in the hole, and my wife told me it was a shame the gators weren't wearing those yellow construction hats. But alligators are so tough already, I argued, they're like a big construction hat.

The youngest boy caught a fish that resembled garbage. Unfortunately, after the fish had swallowed the hook, the pointy end punctured through its eye. This made the boy sad, so an older, freckled boy muscled the fish from him, yanked out the hook, and punctured it through the fish's other eye. Pliny the Elder attested in his *Natural History* that ghosts despise people with freckles, so I whispered to my wife, "Pliny the Elder." She demanded the freckled kid hand over the fish, and she tossed it into the water after removing the hook. My wife was always performing small kindnesses, such as saving fish. As we left, I tried to make her feel better by saying, "We will never have a son who is a bully." And she replied, "I don't care if he's a murderer."

According to the Saxons, the woman who routinely miscarries may be visited by the ghosts of the children she has lost. In the *Lacnunga*, a book of their folk remedies, a charm is suggested: Let the woman who cannot nourish her child take part of her own child's grave, wrap it in black wool, and trade it to merchants, then say, "I sell it, you buy it, this black wool and this seed of grief." The child's grave is the miscarried child.

If you are not my wife, I texted, then who are you?

Were you aware that you can make enough money to pay your mortgage, she texted back, by searching the internet for rich assholes who are too busy to procrastinate? I keep the best results for myself.

What are some of your searches?

How to avoid rectal prolapse. Names for fruit in foreign languages. Words in which the word "wild" is contained. How to hire a clown. Trauma and brain chemistry. The most famous great ape. Guilt from lying to a dementia patient. If you are in an airplane and it crashes, will you feel pain at impact?

Famous great apes, please.

You'll have to pay.

Happy to pay for premium great ape information.

Or you could tell me who you are.

I am a realtor to the damned.

When we beheld the oil paintings of teeth with sexy ladies—models leaning on fillings as on the hoods of cars, chanteuses in sequined gowns draped on the lunar landscapes of crowns—I asked my wife, "What the fuck?"

"This was a psychopath," she replied.

"Should we check under the floor for bodies?"

"Knock yourself out, but you know how I feel about mouths. Dentists should be forbidden from putting illustrations of smiling teeth holding toothbrushes on their awnings. Everybody acts like it's normal, but it would be like if you went to the bathroom in a restaurant and the sign was an overjoyed bladder pissing in a toilet. I have questions. Do the teeth have teeth? Do they floss?"

The paintings were donated to charity, except for the one we kept—our favorite redhead in a red bikini. She hung over our sectional and made an excellent conversation piece for guests. We proposed names: Leonora, Gertrude, Remedios, Sylvia, Eileen. Nothing stuck, so we ended up referring to her as *Portrait of a Woman with Second Molar.*

In the pantheon of ghosts, there is a veritable pageant of unearthly ladies. Should they be categorized by region? By era? By age? (It is indecorous to query a lady, especially a spectral lady, how old she is.) As the attendant pulled down the white sheet over my wife's face in the hospital morgue and I confirmed, "Yes, that is her," I remembered those many brides filled with rage behind their ephemeral veils. But they shouldn't be summed up merely by the hue of their muslin and lace.

Let's not be coy, I texted. *I'd like to take you out on a date.*

How about the Denny's in Siesta Key?

Denny's it is. I will treat you to a Denver omelet.

I don't want to be committed to Denver.

Please, feel free to choose any metropolitan-area omelet that you crave. But before we meet, can you confirm whether or not you are my wife?

Guy, I got a new plan, and my carrier randomly assigned me this number.

As I conducted my test of the taps to determine whether the plumbing was functional in the Reluctant Gambler's condo, we learned we were in the direct path of the hurricane. The Reluctant Gambler was dubbed the Reluctant Gambler on account of his stacks and stacks of scratch-off lottery tickets that weren't scratched off. Hurricane Frida had altered course almost impossibly—or quite possibly, in keeping with the capricious habits of hurricanes. My wife and I hid in a walk-in closet with a dialysis machine that was also in hiding. We hoped to wait out the storm the way we endured our open houses: with ghost stories.

Saint Louis of France, my wife read, was a very religious king. Due to his piety or simply because he was nice, he donated a manor near Paris to monks from the Order of Saint Bruno. The monks were not resentful in the slightest that right next door was the Palace of Vauvert, a residence of superior majesty. Vauvert didn't have a reputation for ghosts, yet after the monks arrived, reports circulated that it was home to the ghost of a bearded man in robes who shrieked obscenities. When word of these goings-on reached the king, he was appalled and inquired if the monks had heard about the phantom neckbeard. The monks expressed their sympathetic shock and disgust and promised the king that, in exchange for taking up residence, they would exorcise the ghost. Relieved, Louis had a deed drawn up that designated the Palace of Vauvert the official abode of the monks of Saint Bruno. The devoted monks, if they ever did encounter the ghost, at least did not complain.

"Pretending to be ghosts could be our side hustle," I said to my wife.

"I'm not sure anyone will believe we're a couple of thirteenth century monks," she replied.

Hurricane Frida made landfall while my wife continued to read, and I offered her my senses if not my interest. The tides were rising and rising—I was convinced that we would drown in that condo, though in my mind the dialysis machine floated peacefully out the front door and into the canals. Ultimately, the storm spared the condo of the Reluctant Gambler, but the rest of the block was the picture of a haunting. I kept quiet and didn't mention again how it was lucky we didn't have children, how the world was getting worse, the floods hotter, the summers higher. My wife was a cheerful person until confronted with the suffering of the vulnerable or crushing desire, at which point she became cheerful beyond comfort. She would probably bring up Lewes Lavater's lament, in 1572, in *Of Ghostes and Spirites Walking by Nyght*: "The world waxeth worse and worse. Men are now more impudent, more dould, more couetous, and more wicked, than euer they were in times past, and their ghostes doe but followe in deede."

At Denny's in Siesta Key, I wore a rose in my lapel like an idiot, requested a booth, and drank a cup of coffee. I drank another cup of coffee, and I got the jitters. The woman who had my dead wife's phone number didn't appear, and I wished my wife were there to read me ghost stories while I waited for the woman who had her number.

I'm in a booth at Denny's, and I'm wearing a rose in my lapel like an idiot, I texted.

I'm sorry, she texted back. *I've been gathering up my courage to leave my bed and come to Denny's. The truth is that I moved here to get away from someone, someone who hurt me very badly. I just can't meet a strange man right now, I'm sorry.*

I understood, I told her. Don't be sorry.

The ancient Greeks divided ghosts into several types: *idolon, aoroi, ataphoi, umbra, larva, lemure, imago, plasma, effigy, mane, muliebris*. Canadians have their *windigos* and the Inuit their *angiaks*. The Japanese, their voluptuous, vulpine *kokitenos*. As long as there is space and time and real estate, there will be ghosts. There are ghosts who distress, ghosts who simply wish to impress, and ghosts here to redress their crimes; there are poltergeist ghosts who play pranks, housekeeper ghosts who clean without thanks, avaricious ghosts who rob banks; there are ghosts of the theater, ghosts of the opera, ghosts of the cinema; there are ghostly miners digging in coal-stained overalls; there are ghostly bakers preparing ectoplasmic croissants; there are ghostly surgeons performing ghostly operations; there are ghosts inhabiting ghost towns in the American West; there are ghostly traveling circuses and ghosts on skates circling roller rinks, and gleeful ghosts sledding down wintry slopes; there are ghosts dancing across the floors of the Ozone Disco in the Philippines who were dancing in the club when it collapsed; there are ghostly hotel guests and ghostly bellhops; there are ghosts in tennis matches, the ghost of a jockey galloping on top his horse at Happy Valley Racecourse in Hong Kong, and the ghost of Andrew Irvine, who perished ascending Everest in 1924 and has stayed to assist struggling mountaineers; there are ghostly deep-sea divers who succumbed to the bends, strapped onto ghostly oxygen tanks; there are ghosts who operate ghostly ships, dirigibles, and trains; there is my text-message ghost; then there is the ghost of my wife.

We didn't discuss what we would be like as ghosts ourselves, or, when one of us died, if we would return to haunt the bereaved spouse. I imagine I would be a rather bumbling spirit, unsure whether to stay or leave, and in the interim I'd try to be helpful by organizing the pantry or tossing junk mail. My wife, however, would not have opted to become a ghost—she was the decider in our relationship—but by refusing to let go of our ghost hobby I was turning her into one, an entity in my mind that was and was not my wife. A memory is altered each time it is recollected, so whenever I long for my wife I lose her more and more. That's another fact in support of the existence of ghosts: for what could be more ghostly than missing someone so intensely that you can no longer remember her as she was?

not setsuko

Unlike most mothers, I gave birth to my daughter Setsuko not once, but twice. The first was a sunny day in the middle of summer, and she came without complication. It was an easy, joyful birth. The second was a stormy afternoon ten years later to the date. I was induced in the same private hospital, under the care of the same doctor—with the same laser-whitened smile, he had apparently delivered the babies for some of L.A.'s most famous actresses. That time, however, Setsuko was taken out of me by emergency caesarean. She was breeched, and the umbilical cord was suffocating her slowly, knotted around her neck. Ever since, I have worried about the effect this may have had upon her reborn psyche.

In a few weeks, she will turn nine—the last day of her first life—and I am trying to prepare her for it. Before, she stood four feet four inches tall and registered fifty-five on the scale.

Now she only reaches to four feet three-and-a-quarter inches and weighs more than sixty pounds. This is not satisfactory. Every morning I wake her early for a workout and take her measurements.

"Rise and shine, sleepyhead!" I say in my most singsong motherly voice. She groans and burrows stubbornly under the covers, but I don't take no for an answer. Children need their parents to be authority figures and to instruct them how to stay disciplined.

"Sixty-two pounds." I sigh in disappointment, recording the number. "Let's get you running."

I set the treadmill at a challenging incline and work her up to a healthy sweat. "Faster, Coco!" I encourage over the thumping of her shoes.

"No!" she shouts and climbs off the machine. She retreats to a corner and hugs her legs to her chest. Her hair falls over her face. "I'm not fat."

"Honey," I reply, kneeling beside her, "I know that, but you don't look the way you used to look. You were so pretty and popular. Don't you want to have that again?"

She raises her mournful eyes to meet mine and nods.

"Then hop back up there!"

After the physical exercises, I put Setsuko through her mental paces.

"Do you remember what you wanted to be when you grew up before you were nine the first time?" I ask.

"Did I still want to be a professional ballerina?"

"Not anymore." I frown. "If you get it right, I'll let you have a treat."

She scrunches her face in concentration, then brightens and pops her eyes wide open.

"A vet!" she cries. "I wanted to be a veterinarian."

"Good!" I say. "Do you remember why?"

"Because of Miruku," she says. I take out a packet of mochi from the cupboard and pass her a rice bonbon filled with red bean paste. She snatches it from my fingers. Our cat, Miruku, as if on cue, jumps up on Coco's lap. "Miru!" Coco squeals and covers the furry forehead with kisses.

Tonight, I am going to go through with the Miruku incident, no more excuses. For what would be her final Christmas, we gifted Setsuko with a completely white kitten. She doted on the animal and rushed home from school to cuddle her and play catch-the-fabric-mouse. Mistakenly, we let Miruku wander outside. Our house is on coastal property in Malibu, so we thought she would merely chase gulls and dig up hermit crabs by the water. When she didn't come home one night, we went scouring the beach. But living by the ocean also means that we're next to the Pacific Coast Highway, and in the morning, a neighbor brought us Miruku's slender body. The cat had been hit by a car. Setsuko cradled the kitten to her chest, the white coat matted and soiled, and cried. It broke my heart. I knelt down, enveloped them both in my arms, and cried, too. I promised my Coco I would get her another kitten. Of course, I never had the chance.

It's regrettable that our restagings haven't been totally consistent. For example, when Setsuko number one was seven, we went snowboarding at Big Bear. She was having so much fun, gliding effortlessly along the slopes, until she had a bad spill and fractured her wrist. I wanted to create this event anew somehow, but my husband, Wyatt, expressly forbade it. Still, I comfort myself by recalling that I had my second Setsuko wear a cast around her undamaged arm for six weeks anyway. To compensate for the missing memory, I frequently have her narrate the event from start to finish and test her on the details. My hope is that if she repeats the story long enough, the fiction will become her reality.

"Tell me about the day at Big Bear," I say. We're overdue for a full recitation.

"We drove out of the city and up a mountain road. It was afternoon when we got to the lodge. We strapped into our boots and boards, and a ski instructor showed us some moves on a bunny hill. I fell over a bunch of times but eventually figured out how to keep my balance."

"Fine," I say, "but I want specifics. Use your five senses. How cold was it? What color was the snow?"

"The snow was white like Miruku but almost blue. It was really cold, so cold my toes went numb, and I had to go eat french fries and warm up inside."

"Continue," I reply.

"I was nervous at first, but after lunch I wasn't nervous. I wanted to try a hard trail like the older kids. I boarded a lift to a black diamond. I was doing okay, but then I hit an icy patch. I fell and landed on my wrist. I couldn't stand back up, it hurt so bad. Some nice men came and took me down the hill on a stretcher."

"Well done, Setsuko," I say. She flashes me a goofy smile, showing the gap between her two front teeth. It seems to me she always used to smile a lot more. I'll have to correct her about that later. "I'm so proud of you, I'm going to let you have another mochi."

She gently cups the dough and smells it in pleasure before taking a bite.

"You must be looking forward to your birthday," I add. "You'll be allowed to eat as much candy as you want."

"I'm more excited for my tenth birthday," she says under her breath, but it's not lost on me. We've been restaging her parties for so many years that I will hardly know what to do when I have to organize one from scratch.

"Now go practice your instrument," I say.

While Coco is distracted with scales on the violin, I grab Miruku, sneak out the back door, and set her in the middle of our driveway. I climb into Wyatt's convertible and slide my key into the ignition. In the rearview mirror, I watch the cat sniffing at the ground. To psych myself up and calm my shaky nerves, I rev the engine a couple times. "It's okay," I say, "you're doing this for your daughter." The tires scream as I run over the animal with the sports car. I check my work. The pelvis and hind legs appear to be broken, but Miruku is alive, yowling in pain.

"Shit," I mutter and get back in the convertible. I want to cry, but I need to stay strong. Sometimes you have to do bad things in order to manifest good things. During the second attempt, I'm fairly confident I feel the wheels crunch the skull against concrete. I hide the body in a trash bag in the garage and wait for my husband to come home.

Before the rebirth, Wyatt demanded I go into therapy. It was one of his conditions, he said. Initially, he wanted me to join him in his bereavement group, but I declined. If our baby was returning to us, there was nothing to grieve. When I began describing plans for restagings, my counselor was curious as to why I couldn't let Setsuko make new memories. Did she have kids? I asked. She didn't. Well, I explained, one of the frightening things you learn when you become a parent is that you can't protect your children from life. Anything can go wrong: they can slip on the bars of the jungle gym and get a concussion, they can die of SIDS in the night, they can be kidnapped. The only power you have is to give them the best chance possible. Could I control everything that happened to Setsuko? No, I couldn't, but since she used to be such a delightful little girl, so exuberant and charming, I was determined to provide her with the memories that made her that way.

Besides, I said, it wasn't that strange anymore for parents to seek a duplication. Several celebrity couples have done so, like they showed in that documentary. Why shouldn't I?

That answer seemed to placate both her and my husband. What I didn't say was that I also plain miss my daughter, and whenever I see a flash of the old Setsuko in her new incarnation, I feel a surge of love in my chest. Yes, I think, this is how it is supposed to be. Here she is, my Setsuko.

When Wyatt comes in, I can't wait to tell him my news. "I did it!" I exclaim. "Everything's ready. By tomorrow, the Miruku memory will be in place." His features pinch together. The resemblance is uncannily similar to the face Setsuko makes when I scold her for not behaving like herself.

"When you refer to 'the Miruku memory,' what does that mean?" he asks.

"I'll show you," I say.

We go into the garage, where I peel open the plastic lip of the trash bag. At the sight of the mangled feline, his face shifts from skepticism to numb disbelief. It's not the response I had hoped for: Like father, like daughter. Wyatt can occasionally become contrary. Alas, this is an instance where he'll need some soothing.

"We agreed you had to check with me before restaging something that would hurt Setsuko," he says.

"We already know she gets over it without that much trouble."

"That's not the point," he replies.

Then he adds, "What else have you done to her that you're keeping from me?"

"Nothing!" I protest. "And I'm telling you now about Miruku."

"After it's too late to stop you."

"Don't be angry," I say, hurrying after him as he walks back into the house. "I apologize for not telling you beforehand, but I figured you'd be glad our daughter is almost our daughter again."

"I can't be there for this one."

"The important episodes of our Coco's life are unfolding and you're missing them."

"It's not like I haven't seen it before."

Hearing our voices, Setsuko skips out of her room. "Daddy!" she cries and leaps into his arms. "Hi, angel," Wyatt says, nuzzles his nose against her scalp, and holds her tight. I can tell he's sad that he's aware of what's in store for her soon but she is not. The scene is exquisitely tender. How I yearn to participate once more in such spontaneous loving moments. We've waited so long to be a family.

That evening, after Wyatt has departed and it's just Setsuko and me doing dishes, I compose my best worried expression, then say, "You know, I'm a bit concerned. It's well past dinner, and I haven't seen a glimpse of Miruku."

"I'll find her!" Setsuko replies and peers under couches and beds. When about twenty minutes have elapsed, she becomes panicked. Her face is exactly as stricken as it was years ago. As anticipated, we gear up with windbreakers and flashlights and search the beach.

"Miruku! Miruku!" my Setsuko calls into the dark. She can't stop sobbing. She loved the cat the second time as much as the first.

"Darling, let's give it a rest," I say. "I'm sure she'll be home by morning."

Wyatt set up his production company shortly before we got engaged. His dream was to direct ethereal art house films, but he got sidelined into producing low-budget horror movies to avoid bankruptcy. We met while he was still in graduate school. I was waiting tables and auditioning like mad. His casting notice said he was in need of a Japanese actress, so I sent in my headshot. He seemed let down when he called me in and discovered I couldn't speak the language, but I landed the role regardless. Over the years, he's tried to teach it to me, but I found the grammar too different from English. He has also suggested that we book a trip to Japan and trace my lineage, but I wasn't interested in the scheme. My real family is my adopted parents in Orange County. They christened me Karen. Wyatt was the one who thought it was cute to refer to me as Kyoko. Fortunately, when Setsuko came along, she showed a more avid interest in picking up words and phrases. The downside is that the two of them often laugh and chatter together in a tongue I will never know.

At some point, Wyatt shifted his focus entirely on the horror films. I think that since he used to study Kabuki theater in Tokyo, it wasn't too difficult for him to channel his vision from one genre into the other. Right around Setsuko's rebirth, he became obsessed with the *yurei*, vengeful ghosts who are trapped in the physical world on account of their violent deaths. They appear in white funeral attire with a tangled mane of hair. Almost always they are young girls. Wyatt is currently shooting what he's said might be his opus. Reeling over the recent abduction and murder of their daughter in Los Angeles, an American couple travels to a rural village in Japan to try to move on and save their faltering marriage. It is there, in their rented house, that they encounter the *yurei* of Yumi, who had been strangled by a visiting stranger when she was nine years old. She bombards their minds with images of her death. Only after releasing her into the spirit world can they make peace with the loss of their own daughter. I wouldn't feel so weird about the whole thing if Wyatt hadn't begged me, this once, for Setsuko to play the part of the ghostly child. He so rarely invokes his veto that I felt obligated to comply. I can't risk him becoming frustrated and halting my restagings altogether; I know what he's like, as a director, when he doesn't get his way. And little girls are always dressing up and pretending to be other people—how much harm could it do?

Lying by myself in bed until the early hours of the morning, I find I am bursting with too much anticipation over the upcoming Miruku scene to sleep. I can't wait even a few more hours to break the news. I dig the bloody cat out of the trash bag in the garage, ring our doorbell, and shake Setsuko awake.

"The neighbors found our Miruku," I say, presenting the carcass. "She must have been hit by a car."

As before, Setsuko takes the cat from me, cradles it to her chest, and sobs. I put my arms around her. "Oh, precious one," I whisper, "I promise I'll get you another kitten." I feel my tears falling on her hair. It is perfect.

"It doesn't matter," Setsuko replies, surprising me. That's not like last time at all. "No kitten will ever be the same as Miruku."

I allow Setsuko to sleep through her workout the next day until we need to leave for our tedious commute into Hollywood. I usually run errands or have lunch while they're filming, but today, for whatever reason—an ominous hunch—I stay. Emerging from the makeup department with ratted locks and powdered skin, Setsuko really looks like a corpse. Gaffers and grips buzz about, checking that the proper gels are on the proper lights. The actors show up drinking lattes. Slowly, the scene of the hour comes together: The couple, fresh off the plane and unpacking their things, make love while the *yurei* watches from the bedroom doorway. The wife-actress is predictably young and rather attractive, shining hair cascading past the waistline of her silk robe embroidered with cherry blossoms.

"Quiet on set," the assistant director says. "Action."

Giggling, the wife runs into the frame, with the husband in close pursuit. She grabs a pillow and hits him with it on the shoulder. He tugs the robe's sash, slides a hand underneath it, then slides another hand into that gorgeous hair. They tongue-kiss with great enthusiasm until she leads him to bed, where they tumble in a heap of passion. In a minute, Setsuko emerges into the doorway.

"*Koroshiteyaru*," she utters softly. There are tracks in her cake foundation.

"Cut!" Wyatt yells. "Not bad for a first take. I'd like it to be slightly less playful and more hesitant. Remember, you've recently buried your daughter and are desperate to reconnect. Setsuko, you're a natural. Do it like that again. Okay, angel?"

"Yes, Daddy," my spectral girl says, eager to please.

The set is restored to its original state. The husband, on touching his wife in subsequent takes, is timid, almost fearful. They act it out over and over to get the full coverage: the wide shots, medium shots, close-ups, over-the-shoulder shots. When Wyatt calls a break for lunch at noon, the crew bustles with activity, but I swear I see him approach the wife and tuck stray hair behind an ear with a caress trailing to her chin. He's a director, she's his leading lady, I remind myself. This kind of passing flirtation happens all the time.

When they wrap, Wyatt remains at the studio to review the dailies. I drive Setsuko home in endless rush-hour traffic. She refuses to break the monotony and won't return my gaze or even speak to me. She's still upset about the cat.

"Coco, what does '*Koroshiteyaru*' mean?" I ask in curiosity.

"I will kill you both," she replies at last.

I wonder how many memories I have left to give my daughter, so I comb through the file I've kept of school exercises, drawings, and her diary—the lock of which I picked after we had to say goodbye for a while. In nostalgia, I review the entries of Coco learning how to ride a bike, cooking marshmallows over a fire on our Yosemite camping trip, receiving her first kiss at a pool party. The kiss I restaged with a boy actor matching Setsuko's adorable confession of her crush, only to discover afterward that second Setsuko had already been kissed behind the soda machines in kindergarten. I suppose there's bound to be some mismatches. It makes me wish I had devised a test of some kind to determine whether or not Setsuko is who she's supposed to be. I tell myself that perfection is impossible, but if I try to get things as close as I can for her, she'll have the best chance of returning to me. I'm sure that on her birthday, I'll receive a sign—she'll tell me a secret only the old Setsuko will know, whisper, "I'm back, Mommy," in my ear, even a long-forgotten gesture of hers would be enough.

Finally, the anticipated day arrives, and I've made sure everything is in order. I've rewrapped her toys gifted a decade past. There's a bubble maker on our deck and a pony will be on the beach. Tables are laden with steamed dumplings and mochi. I tell Setsuko she's not to go out of my sight.

One by one, the guests show up and change into their bathing suits. Boys and girls laugh and scream and splash each other in the ocean, but my Coco ignores them. She seems transfixed by the machine wearily cranking out iridescent globes that hover indefinitely over Pacific tides. After considerable wrangling, I get the group quieted and gathered in the living room. "How nice," my daughter deadpans after unwrapping an outmoded doll. "Thanks, Jenny." The kids clap and Jenny shrugs. The next present is a metallic robot dog. Setsuko places it on the carpet and presses the on switch. Lights flare up behind the dog's red eyes and demonically glow. Its four limbs wheeze a hydraulic, grinding sound as it walks forward and pauses every ten seconds to issue forth a series of identical, soulless barks. Wyatt steps outside to talk on his cell. When it's time to sing "Happy Birthday," I try to get him to join in, but he waves me away with a flick of his wrist. I bring out a chocolate cake from the kitchen, and the rest of us bellow out the tune to my daughter.

"Now make a wish," I tell her. The candles paint her face an ominous crimson. She closes her eyes tight, then pops them wide open and blows out the flames.

"The pony has arrived out back," I say. "You can line up for a ride!" There is cheering and clapping and clamoring to get out of the house. Only Setsuko lingers.

"Mommy," she says, sidling up to me. "Do you want to know what I wished for?"

"What, baby?" I ask.

Perhaps this is the big moment. I feel the surging inside my chest.

"I thought that since this was the last of my old birthdays that I'm free to be whatever I want." She takes a deep breath. "I decided to tell you I don't want to be a veterinarian when I grow up. I want to be an actress!"

"Don't be silly," I reply. "That's not something you ever would have wanted."

"I changed my mind," she pouts.

"No," I say. "That's final. Why don't you join your friends?"

"I hate you!" she shouts and storms the steps to where the pony and its trainer are pacing the same track of sand, a different child in the saddle every other pass. When she nears the group, they howl in laughter as the pony kinks up its tail and poops. Like something out of a nightmare, I watch Setsuko dart forward, pick up the shit, and hurl it at the other nine-year-olds. They howl in disgust and scatter toward the water while Coco grins as if possessed.

"Setsuko!" I scold, hurrying to the beach and grabbing her by the arms. "What do you think you're doing?"

"Leave me alone!" She tries to wriggle from my hold, but I won't let go.

"I hope you're aware of how much trouble you're in, young lady," I say. She stops struggling. Either cake or manure streaks one of her cheeks.

"You promised I wouldn't have to do everything you say anymore," she whines. "You said you didn't know what was supposed to happen next."

"I still expect you to behave like my daughter," I say. "Don't you want to save poor kitties like Miruku?"

"You killed Miruku!"

"It was an accident. Miruku was hit by a car."

"You're lying. I know that you did it."

"Please, Coco," I say, sinking to my knees. "Show me that you're here, my darling. Give me some indication that the little girl I see before me is the Setsuko I love."

"Do you want to know what he did to me?" she asks.

"What do you mean?"

"It was worse than you can imagine. I bit and scratched, but he was too strong."

"You don't know what you're talking about."

"When he got bored, he put his hairy hands on my throat and squeezed until I died."

"Be quiet! You're grounded."

"But I was glad that I was dead, since it meant I would never have to see my awful mom who didn't care about me ever again!"

In shock, I release her and she flees, and I lay my forehead on the sand, trying to regain my composure while my whole body shakes. It was the one memory meant to be lost forever. What if this is my proof that she has returned and is punishing me for not being a more careful mother? No, it can't be. Setsuko has never met her abductor in this incarnation. The man who stole my daughter from her ninth birthday party and discarded her in a dumpster on the corner of Melrose and La Brea is serving a life sentence without the possibility of parole. As few facts as possible were explained to her about what happened that day. I'm not sure how she put this much of the story together. I must have erred, allowed too many changes from her former childhood. Wyatt's project also couldn't have helped matters. It's given her some morbid ideas. I brush myself off and bitterly prepare to confront him about it.

Ever the director, he hasn't yet gotten off the phone. I motion for him to finish the conversation. He knows when he can and can't ignore me. He cuts short his call.

"Setsuko's out of the film," I say. "She's becoming unmanageable."

"I need at least another week to capture the ending."

"She just threw her death in my face."

"I swear I haven't said a word about it."

"She has to settle into her identity, and she's too vulnerable to suggestion. I can't allow more acting in her regimen."

"Unfortunately, I'm unable to replace her at this stage. I'd have to reshoot too much of the script. It's not in the budget."

"So rewrite the remainder of the script."

"I've been meaning to talk to you anyway, Kyoko. The actress playing the wife has to take a leave of absence, but that puts us in a tough spot. I was hoping I could ask you to fill in. Then you could also keep an eye on Setsuko until we've wrapped."

"You're unwilling to recast our daughter, but you can swap one wife for another without a problem?"

"We got the wife's coverage for her remaining scenes with the *yurei*, but we need Setsuko's close-ups and reversals. Since you're the same height and build, it should work if we only see you from behind."

"Recast Setsuko, and I'll do it. She's in heavy makeup. No one will notice."

"Kyoko, no. This isn't up to you."

He had been remarkably tolerant of how I had chosen to raise Setsuko, Wyatt continued. Perhaps too tolerant. But how do you explain to your little girl what happened to the child who came before her? My way might actually be the kindest, he had thought, by gradually introducing her to facts and memories until she was old enough to understand. Especially since her older sister was her duplicate—or vice versa. Nevertheless, he couldn't let me sabotage the film that might be his finest achievement. Since our second Setsuko was nine, I had to begin letting go and accepting our daughter for who she is.

"That's pretty hypocritical coming from you," I say. "My name isn't Kyoko. It's Karen. I've never been the woman you've wanted me to be."

"Okay, Karen," Wyatt replies, "that pet name has never bothered you before, but tell me something. What happens now you've run out of Setsuko's memories? There's nothing left to do."

"A pet name isn't usually a common first name from another country," I say, "but to answer your question, Setsuko clearly needs more training. More recitations, plus fresh restagings of crucial memories we didn't get quite right before she's able to come back."

"She never gets to be a regular kid, is that it—until you decide that she's ready to be loved?"

"If that's what it takes, then yes."

Wyatt turns away from me toward the beach so I can't see the face he makes, whether it's one that I have recognized in my daughter, one that I know how to tend to and positively influence.

"I'll tell you what," he says. "Give me one shoot, you as the wife and Setsuko as the ghost daughter, and I'll figure out the rest."

"We're all yours," I say.

Setsuko gloats throughout our morning drive to the studio the next week. She thinks the fact that we're following the routine of exercising then filming means she has defied me and won.

"On my birthday, I told Daddy I wanted to be in movies, too, and he said he would sign me up for an acting class," she says.

"I guess that was before we came to a parental decision," I reply, pulling into the parking lot.

"What decision?" She sounds doubtful, much more docile.

"The decision that after this film is complete, you're done," I say. "No more acting."

I drag my tantruming daughter inside and unload her on the makeup people. Sitting motionless in the company of relative strangers should subdue her anger. I slip into the robe with cherry blossoms and review the sides. The current scene is near the end. The ghost Yumi has become more violent and increasingly corporeal from feeding on the couple's fear. While the husband is away scheduling an exorcism with a local witch doctor, Yumi attempts to strangle the wife in her sleep. Upon emerging as her deceased likeness, Setsuko is dismayed to see me in costume.

"What are you doing?" she asks.

"Your mother will be my wife today," Wyatt replies.

We rehearse the confrontation to ensure it's correct, then we're ready. I recline on the tatami mattress and assume the appearance of absolute repose. "Action!" I hear the patter of Setsuko's slippered feet on the bamboo floor. Her delicate fingers circle around my neck. When she cries in Japanese that she wants me to die, I feign terror and watch her attempt at pantomime strangulation. *"Hayaku Shinde!"*

"Cut," Wyatt yells. "Not bad, but I'm not quite buying it. Setsuko, I'd like more energy from you. Picture how your character must feel being trapped in the past. She wants to take revenge on any living thing that gets to experience a future she will never have."

We repeat the struggle for hours, but Wyatt isn't satisfied. There's a fatigue in Setsuko's performance that only increases with every take. She is no longer invested in her role.

"Maybe we should call it a day," Wyatt says. "Setsuko, I'm beginning to think it's a good thing your mother decided that you're not to pursue acting, since you can't seem to understand the simplest note."

The familiar pinched expression flashes over her pallid features but is immediately repressed. My little ghost is upset. Setsuko walks to her first blocking point. "No," she insists. "I can do it."

"Quiet on set." The assistant director looks tentatively at Wyatt, who is breathing through his hands. "Roll camera."

I listen for Coco's light footsteps, but she is silent. After an indeterminate interval, I sense a hovering warmth. I know she is staring down at my reposed face, waiting to make her move. I wonder if something has gone amiss, since nothing happens. It's then I feel her hands upon me.

"*Hayaku Shinde!*" she screams at a shattering volume. She brings the full weight of her body to bear upon my windpipe. I pop my eyes open and do not recognize my own daughter. She truly seems the malignant spirit of a wounded, forgotten child. I attempt to pry her grip off my throat, but she is steadfast. She's stronger than she looks.

"Cut!" Wyatt yells louder. "Cut! Setsuko, stop!"

Several pairs of arms reach in and pull my daughter from me. She lashes out at the PAs until Wyatt relieves them of their burden. Setsuko wails into his collarbone. "Hush, angel," he murmurs. "It's over." He carries her backstage. After I'm done with my coughing fit, I find them in a dressing room. Wyatt is saying pacifying things in Japanese.

"Why don't you change?" he suggests. "Take Coco and go home."

"We should talk about how we're going to punish her."

"I'll leave that to you," he replies.

Then he adds, "In my opinion, she's had enough punishment."

I wait for a word of sympathy from Wyatt, some indication I'm not on my own and he still considers us a team. He only passes our daughter from his arms to mine, then quickly makes his exit.

I sneak into Setsuko's bedroom that night and watch her sleep. I speculate about whether or not dreaming different dreams would be enough to change a child's personality. In this state, she looks most like my baby, but I know it is a lie. I have failed. The child before me is not Setsuko. Rather, she is a perversion of my daughter, neither alive nor dead.

Close to midnight, I get a call from Wyatt. He wants a divorce. I beg him to reconsider. What happened on set was traumatic, I say, but we can figure everything out. I can go to therapy again. Wyatt and I can go to couples' therapy. We can put Setsuko in therapy. We can all go into therapy.

"I'm sorry, Karen," he replies, "but it's too late for therapy. We should have ended this years ago." Coco's meltdown during the film, the cat. It's been too much.

"If she can show me that her memories have taken hold," I say, "we can have our family back good as new."

"Maybe you were scrutinizing Setsuko so closely for a sign that you missed it."

Anyway, it doesn't matter. Wyatt is in love. The wife-actress is pregnant. She said she couldn't work with him, that it was too painful, unless something changed. He was agonized over what to do, but now he's certain. And if I was honest with myself, did I really want our family back? Though he will, of course, share custody of Setsuko, moving on will be better for all of us.

Wyatt's things disappear from the house. School starts. The master bedroom becomes littered with the pictures and papers from my first Setsuko. I keep her journal next to my pillow. I should be more attentive to second Setsuko, but I don't have the heart. Coco is out of control. Her teachers complain that she bullies the other children. I visit the principal's office. The principal shows me drawings my daughter has done in art class. Each depicts a Japanese girl getting killed in a most macabre fashion: blown apart, poisoned, drowned, set on fire, disemboweled, hung from the rafters of a barn while the farm animals look on in fear. Across the bottom of one of the pages is scrawled the words, "I want to die, die, die, die, die!"

I pick Setsuko up after my meeting with the principal, but I don't want to head home. I know we should talk about the drawings. Instead, I ask her what she'd like to do. I'll take her anywhere she wants. We drive to the Santa Monica Pier. The chintzy restaurants and malodorous hot dog stands and mobile vendors selling ice cream are clotted with families. Surfers and waves practice their ability to crash. Garbage roiling in the water tosses against the sand. Teens blast pop songs from portable stereos and rub each other with suntan lotion. It occurs to me they are the age Setsuko should be, while she is stuck at nine. I think of Wyatt's growing child, becoming more of a distinct person by the day. Will he love it more than he loves our little girl? I let Coco go wild. Whenever she asks for something to eat, I hand over the money. She plays arcade games and boards every mini-ride, some of them several times, before she tires.

At dusk, we ride the Ferris wheel. The white metal cars turn around and around as we watch the sunset over the northern hills. The screams and laughter, the sigh of the tide are just echoes up high. Setsuko bounces from one side of the enclosure to the other while eating an ice-cream cone. She leaves drips of it in her passing, a trail of hardening sugar. I feel something aching, something surging inside of me, then subsiding again. I want to cry, but I need to stay strong. Or maybe that's no longer true.

"Mommy," Setsuko says with a happy smile, "I think I'm going to remember this day forever!"

"That's nice, baby," I reply. Unexpectedly, the Ferris wheel stops and we are suspended at the apex of its circle, swinging back and forth in air. I take my daughter's sticky sweet hands in mine.

"Tell me the story," I say.

acknowledgments

I would not have been able to bring this collection into the world without the generosity of the following individuals:

To Eric Chinski, thank you for the faith you have placed in me and my writing. I'm incredibly honored to be one of the authors under your guidance.

To Julia Ringo, it has been such a gift to work with an editor who is so brilliant and attentive as well as so kind. Thank you for helping me to see these stories with new eyes and to shape them into their best possible forms. You are a wonder.

To Cynthia Cannell, I am grateful to have such a dedicated and elegant agent as my advocate. My thanks to you, Charlotte, and Nico at CCLA for your insight and all the opportunities you've made possible for me.

To Diane Williams, I could not have asked for a better mentor, and I cherish the years we've spent working together on *NOON*. I have learned so much about power and concision in fiction from observing how your extraordinary mind approaches editing.

Thank you to my professors at Northwestern University and Columbia School of the Arts for your early support and for helping me to become a better thinker about the craft of writing, with special gratitude to: Brian Bouldrey, Rebecca Curtis, Stuart Dybek, Rivka Galchen, Samantha Gillison, John Keene, Mary Kinzie, Paul La Farge, Sam Lipsyte, Ben Marcus, Tom McCarthy, Eleanor Wilner, and Christian Wiman.

To Andy Yamazaki, thank you for your thoughtful and detailed assistance in translation.

acknowledgments

To Xuan Juliana Wang, your support and care will always be remembered and appreciated.

Thank you to my dearest friends and first readers of this entire collection in its many drafts over the years: Hilary Leichter, JW McCormack, and Mary Roberts. I am in debt to you beyond measure for your notes, your reassurance, and your wisdom.

Thank you to my writing group and the following talented writers who read and offered great insight on many of these stories: Rebekah Bergman, Rita Bullwinkel, Jessamine Chan, Diane Cook, Claudia Cravens, Lee Ellis, Yael Korman, Heather Monley, Wistar Murray, and David Varno.

Thank you to Emily Gref and Grace Ross for their invaluable professional counsel.

Thank you to Joshua Weil, Clare Beams, and my workshop at the Bread Loaf Writers Conference as well as my fellow waiters for becoming such warm friends and readers: 'Pemi Aguda, Dapne Palassi Andreades, Afua Ansong, Taneum Bambrick, Erica Berry, Noah Bogdonoff, Michaela Cowgill, Dolapo Demuren, Jonathan Escoffery, Vince Granata, Taylor Koekkoek, Jaime Lalinde, Grace You Li, Rachel Mannheimer, Alex McElroy, Josha Jay Nathan, Sebastian Paramo, Anne Price, Zoë Ruiz, Laurie Thomas, Morgan Thomas, and De'Shawn Winslow.

To my parents, my deepest gratitude for raising me and giving me the encouragement and hope that I could pursue this dream to become a writer. Thank you for providing me with a home and making my life possible.

To Andrew Parker, thank you for being such a source of strength, for your unwavering belief in me and my career, and for your love.